*Rodgers & Hammerstein Acting Edition*

# Rodgers & Hammerstein's
# Oklahoma!

## Music by
## Richard Rodgers

## Book & Lyrics by
## Oscar Hammerstein II

Based on the play *Green Grow the Lilacs* by
Lynn Riggs

Original Choreography by
Agnes de Mille

D0912585

## CONCORD
THEATRICALS

ISBN 978-0-573-70890-9

www.concordtheatricals.com
www.concordtheatricals.co.uk

---

**FOR PRODUCTION INQUIRIES**

UNITED STATES AND CANADA
info@concordtheatricals.com
1-866-979-0447

UNITED KINGDOM AND EUROPE
licensing@concordtheatricals.co.uk
020-7054-7200

Each title is subject to availability from Concord Theatricals Corp., depending upon country of performance. Please be aware that *OKLAHOMA!* may not be licensed by Concord Theatricals Corp. in your territory. Professional and amateur producers should contact the nearest Concord Theatricals Corp. office or licensing partner to verify availability.

---

This work is published by R&H Theatricals, an imprint of Concord Theatricals Corp.

*OKLAHOMA!* premiered on Broadway at the St. James Theatre on March 31, 1943. The production was directed by Rouben Mamoulian, with choreography by Agnes de Mille, scenic design by Lemuel Ayers, costume design by Miles White, and orchestrations by Russell Bennett. The stage manager was Ted Hammerstein. The cast was as follows:

AUNT ELLER . . . . . . . . . . . . . . . . . . . . . . . . . . . . . . . . . . . . . . . . . . . . . Betty Garde

CURLY . . . . . . . . . . . . . . . . . . . . . . . . . . . . . . . . . . . . . . . . . . . . . . . . Alfred Drake

LAUREY . . . . . . . . . . . . . . . . . . . . . . . . . . . . . . . . . . . . . . . . . . . . . Joan Roberts

IKE SKIDMORE . . . . . . . . . . . . . . . . . . . . . . . . . . . . . . . . . . . . . . . Barry Kelley

FRED . . . . . . . . . . . . . . . . . . . . . . . . . . . . . . . . . . . . . . . . . . . . . . . . . Edwin Clay

SLIM . . . . . . . . . . . . . . . . . . . . . . . . . . . . . . . . . . . . . . . . . . . . . Herbert Rissman

WILL PARKER . . . . . . . . . . . . . . . . . . . . . . . . . . . . . . . . . . . . . . . . . . . Lee Dixon

JUD FRY . . . . . . . . . . . . . . . . . . . . . . . . . . . . . . . . . . . . . . . . . . Howard Da Silva

ADO ANNIE CARNES . . . . . . . . . . . . . . . . . . . . . . . . . . . . . . . . . Celeste Holm

ALI HAKIM . . . . . . . . . . . . . . . . . . . . . . . . . . . . . . . . . . . . . . . . . Joseph Buloff

GERTIE CUMMINGS . . . . . . . . . . . . . . . . . . . . . . . . . . . . . . . . Jane Lawrence

ELLEN / DREAM LAUREY . . . . . . . . . . . . . . . . . . . . . . . . . Katharine Sergava

KATE . . . . . . . . . . . . . . . . . . . . . . . . . . . . . . . . . . . . . . . . . . . . . . . . . . . Ellen Love

SYLVIE . . . . . . . . . . . . . . . . . . . . . . . . . . . . . . . . . . . . . . . . . . . Joan McCracken

ARMINA . . . . . . . . . . . . . . . . . . . . . . . . . . . . . . . . . . . . . . . . . . Kate Friedlich

AGGIE . . . . . . . . . . . . . . . . . . . . . . . . . . . . . . . . . . . . . . . . . . . . . . . Bambi Linn

ANDREW CARNES . . . . . . . . . . . . . . . . . . . . . . . . . . . . . . . . . . Ralph Riggs

CORD ELAM . . . . . . . . . . . . . . . . . . . . . . . . . . . . . . . . . . . . . . . . Owen Martin

JESS / DREAM JUD . . . . . . . . . . . . . . . . . . . . . . . . . . . . . . . George Church

CHALMERS / DREAM CURLY . . . . . . . . . . . . . . . . . . . . . . . . . . . Marc Platt

MIKE . . . . . . . . . . . . . . . . . . . . . . . . . . . . . . . . . . . . . . . . . . . . . . . . . Paul Shiers

JOE . . . . . . . . . . . . . . . . . . . . . . . . . . . . . . . . . . . . . . . . . . . . . . . . George Irving

SAM . . . . . . . . . . . . . . . . . . . . . . . . . . . . . . . . . . . . . . . . . . . . . . Hayes Gordon

ENSEMBLE . . . . . . . . . . . . Diana Adams, Elsie Arnold, Bobby Barrentine, John Baum, Harvey Brown, Kenneth Buffett, Margit De Kova, Jack Dunphy, Nona Feid, Gary Fleming, Ray Harrison, Maria Harriton, Rhoda Hoffman, Edmund Howland, Eric Kristen, Ken Leroy, Suzanne Lloyd, Dorothea McFarland, Carl Nelson, Virginia Oswald, Robert Penn, Vivienne Simon, Faye Smith, Vivian Smith, Billie Zay

# CHARACTERS

AUNT ELLER

CURLY

LAUREY

IKE SKIDMORE

FRED

SLIM

WILL PARKER

JUD FRY

ADO ANNIE CARNES

ALI HAKIM

GERTIE CUMMINGS

ELLEN

KATE

SYLVIE

ARMINA

AGGIE

ANDREW CARNES

CORD ELAM

MIKE

JOE

SAM

# SETTING

Indian Territory (now Oklahoma)

# TIME

Just after the turn of the century

# INCLUSION STATEMENT

In this show, the race of the characters is not pivotal to the plot. We encourage you to consider diversity and inclusion in your casting choices.

# A NOTE ON THE DIALECT

As he crafted *Oklahoma!*, Oscar Hammerstein II sought to capture the way people spoke in the territory when the story takes place. In order to guide the performers – who were schooled in fine elocution in the pre-amplified era – Hammerstein often used dialect. We have maintained the script and lyrics as Hammerstein wrote them, but note that the dialect is meant as a guide rather than as indication of exactly how the words need to be spoken.

# MUSICAL NUMBERS

## ACT I

"Opening Act I: Oh, What A Beautiful Mornin'"..................Curly

"Laurey's Entrance"......................................... Laurey

"The Surrey With The Fringe On Top"........ Curly, Laurey, Aunt Eller

"Kansas City" ................................. Will, Aunt Eller, Boys

"The Surrey With The Fringe On Top (Reprise)".................Curly

"I Cain't Say No".........................................Ado Annie

"I Cain't Say No (Encore)" ...............................Ado Annie

"Entrance Of Ensemble".................. Will, Ado Annie, Ensemble

"Many A New Day" ................................. Laurey & Girls

"Dance & Many A New Day (Reprise)" ................ Laurey & Girls

"It's A Scandal! It's A Outrage!" ............... Ali Hakim, Boys, Girls

"People Will Say We're In Love" ......................Curly & Laurey

"Pore Jud Is Daid" .....................................Curly & Jud

"Lonely Room" ................................................ Jud

"Dream Sequence".................... Laurey, Girls & Dream Figures

(a) "Melos"

(b) "Out Of My Dreams"

(c) "Interlude To Ballet"

(d) "Dream Ballet"

## ACT II

"The Farmer And The Cowman"........ Carnes, Aunt Eller, Curly, Will,
Ado Annie, Slim, Ensemble

"All Er Nuthin'".................. Ado Annie, Will, Two Dancing Girls

"People Will Say We're In Love (Reprise)"..............Curly & Laurey

"Oklahoma"...............................Curly, Laurey, Aunt Eller,
Ike, Fred, Ensemble

"Oklahoma (Encore)" ......................Curly, Laurey, Aunt Eller,
Ike, Fred, Ensemble

"Finale Ultimo"........................................... Company

# ACT I

## Scene One
## The Front Lawn of Laurey's Farmhouse

*(The front lawn of Laurey's farmhouse. "It is a radiant summer morning several years ago, the kind of morning which, enveloping the shapes of earth – men, cattle in a meadow, blades of the young corn, streams – makes them seem to exist now for the first time, their images giving off a golden emanation that is partly true and partly a trick of the imagination, focusing to keep alive a loveliness that may pass away.")*

## [MUSIC NO. 01 "OPENING ACT I – OH, WHAT A BEAUTIFUL MORNIN'"]

*(**AUNT ELLER MURPHY**, a buxom, hearty woman about fifty, is seated behind a wooden, brass-banded churn, looking out over the meadow [which is the audience], a contented look on her face. Like the voice of the morning, a song comes from somewhere, growing louder as the young singer comes nearer.)*

**CURLY.** *(Offstage. He sings casually, with a smile in his voice.)*
THERE'S A BRIGHT, GOLDEN HAZE ON THE MEADOW,
THERE'S A BRIGHT, GOLDEN HAZE ON THE MEADOW.
THE CORN IS AS HIGH AS A ELEPHANT'S EYE,
AN' IT LOOKS LIKE IT'S CLIMBIN' CLEAR UP TO THE SKY.

*(On this last line, **CURLY** saunters on and stands outside the gate to the front yard. He is joyful and happy.)*

**CURLY**.

OH, WHAT A BEAUTIFUL MORNIN',
OH, WHAT A BEAUTIFUL DAY.
I GOT A BEAUTIFUL FEELIN'
EV'RYTHIN'S GOIN' MY WAY.

*(He opens the gate and walks over to the porch, obviously singing for the benefit of someone inside the house. **AUNT ELLER** looks straight ahead, elaborately ignoring **CURLY**.)*

ALL THE CATTLE ARE STANDIN' LIKE STATUES,
ALL THE CATTLE ARE STANDIN' LIKE STATUES.
THEY DON'T TURN THEIR HEADS AS THEY SEE ME RIDE
    BY,
BUT A LITTLE BROWN MAV'RICK IS WINKIN' HER EYE.

*(He crosses to up right of **AUNT ELLER**.)*

OH, WHAT A BEAUTIFUL MORNIN',
OH, WHAT A BEAUTIFUL DAY.
I GOT A BEAUTIFUL FEELIN'
EV'RYTHIN'S GOIN' MY WAY.

*(He comes up behind **AUNT ELLER**, leans over, and startles her with a poke in the ribs and shouts in her ear.)*

Hi, Aunt Eller!

**AUNT ELLER**. Skeer me to death! Whut're you doin' around here?

**CURLY**. Come a-singin' to you.

*(Strolling a few steps away.)*

ALL THE SOUNDS OF THE EARTH ARE LIKE MUSIC –
ALL THE SOUNDS OF THE EARTH ARE LIKE MUSIC.
THE BREEZE IS SO BUSY IT DON'T MISS A TREE,
AND A OLE WEEPIN' WILLER IS LAUGHIN' AT ME!

OH, WHAT A BEAUTIFUL MORNIN',
OH WHAT A BEAUTIFUL DAY.

I GOT A BEAUTIFUL FEELIN'
EV'RYTHIN'S GOIN' MY WAY...
OH, WHAT A BEAUTIFUL DAY!

> (**AUNT ELLER** *resumes churning.* **CURLY** *looks wistfully up at the windows of the house, then turns back to* **AUNT ELLER.***)*

**AUNT ELLER.** If I wasn't a ole womern, and if you wasn't so young and smart-alecky – why, I'd marry you and git you to set around at night and sing to me.

**CURLY.** No, you wouldn't neither. Cuz I wouldn't marry you ner none of yer kinfolks, I could he'p it.

> *(He crosses up to the porch.)*

**AUNT ELLER.** *(Wisely.)* Oh, none of my kinfolks, huh?

**CURLY.** *(Raising his voice so that Laurey will hear if she is inside the house.)* And you c'n tell 'em that, all of 'm includin' that niece of your'n, Miss Laurey Williams!

> (**AUNT ELLER** *continues to churn.* **CURLY** *comes down to her and speaks deliberately.)*

Aunt Eller, if you was to tell me whur Laurey was at – whur would you tell me she was at?

**AUNT ELLER.** I wouldn't tell you a-tall. Fer as fer as I c'n make out, Laurey ain't payin' you no heed.

**CURLY.** So, she don't take to me much, huh?

> *(He crosses up left behind* **AUNT ELLER.***)*

Whur'd you git sich a uppity niece 'at wouldn't pay no heed to me? Who's the best bronc buster in this yere territory?

**AUNT ELLER.** You, I bet.

**CURLY.** And the best bull-dogger in seventeen counties? Me, that's who! And looky here, I'm handsome, ain't I?

**AUNT ELLER.** Purty as a pitcher.

**CURLY.** Curly-headed, ain't I? And bow-legged from the saddle fer God knows how long, ain't I?

> *(He bows his legs.)*

**AUNT ELLER.** Couldn't stop a pig in the road.

**CURLY.** Well, whut else does she want then, the damn she-mule?

> (*He crosses down left.*)

**AUNT ELLER.** I don't know. But I'm shore sartin' it ain't you. Who you takin' to the Box Social tonight?

**CURLY.** Ain't thought much about it.

**AUNT ELLER.** Bet you come over to ast Laurey.

**CURLY.** Whuff I did?

**AUNT ELLER.** You astin' me too? I'll wear my fascinator.

**CURLY.** Yeow, you too!

### [MUSIC NO. 02 "LAUREY'S ENTRANCE"]

**LAUREY.** (*Offstage.*)

OH, WHAT A BEAUTIFUL MORNIN'

> (**CURLY** *crosses to the edge of the porch steps and leans against the porch post.* **LAUREY** *enters, carrying an apron.*)

OH, WHAT A BEAUTIFUL DAY.

> (*Spoken as she gives* **CURLY** *a brief glance.*)

Oh, I thought you was somebody.

> (*She resumes singing, crosses to clothesline, and hangs up the apron.*)

I GOT A BEAUTIFUL FEELIN'
EV'RYTHIN'S GOIN' MY WAY.

> (*Spoken as she comes down to* **AUNT ELLER.**)

Is this all that's come a-callin' and it a'ready ten o'clock of a Sattidy mornin'?

**CURLY.** You knowed it was me 'fore you opened the door.

**LAUREY.** No sich of a thing.

**CURLY.** You did, too! You heared my voice and knowed it was me.

**LAUREY.** I heared a voice a-talkin' nimbly along with Aunt Eller. And heared someone a-singin' like a bullfrog in a pond.

**CURLY**. You knowed it was me, so you set in there a-thinkin' up sump'n mean to say. I'm a good mind not to ast you to the Box Social.

> (**AUNT ELLER** *rises, crosses to clothesline, takes down quilt, folds it, puts it on porch.*)

**LAUREY**. If you did ast me, I wouldn't go with you. Besides, how'd you take me? You ain't bought a new buggy with red wheels onto it, have you?

**CURLY**. No, I ain't.

**LAUREY**. And a spankin' team with their bridles all jinglin'?

**CURLY**. No.

> (**AUNT ELLER** *crosses to rocker and sits.*)

**LAUREY**. 'Spect me to ride on behind ole Dun, I guess. You better ast that ole Cummin's girl you've tuck sich a shine to, over acrost the river.

**CURLY**. If I was to ast you, they'd be a way to take you, Miss Laurey Smarty.

**LAUREY**. Oh, they would?

### [MUSIC NO. 03 "THE SURREY WITH THE FRINGE ON TOP"]

> (**CURLY** *now proceeds to stagger* **LAUREY** *with an idea. But she doesn't let on at first how she is "tuck up" with it.* **AUNT ELLER** *is the one who falls like a ton of bricks immediately and helps* **CURLY** *try to sell it to* **LAUREY**.*)

**CURLY**.

> WHEN I TAKE YOU OUT TONIGHT WITH ME,
> HONEY, HERE'S THE WAY IT'S GOIN' TO BE;
> YOU WILL SET BEHIND A TEAM OF SNOW-WHITE HORSES
> IN THE SLICKEST GIG YOU EVER SEE!

**AUNT ELLER**. Lands!

**CURLY**.

> CHICKS AND DUCKS AND GEESE BETTER SCURRY
> WHEN I TAKE YOU OUT IN THE SURREY,
> WHEN I TAKE YOU OUT IN THE SURREY

WITH THE FRINGE ON TOP!

WATCH THET FRINGE AND SEE HOW IT FLUTTERS
WHEN I DRIVE THEM HIGH-STEPPIN' STRUTTERS!
NOSEY-POKES'LL PEEK THRU THEIR SHUTTERS
AND THEIR EYES WILL POP!

THE WHEELS ARE YELLER, THE UPHOLSTERY'S BROWN,
THE DASHBOARD'S GENUINE LEATHER,
WITH ISINGLASS CURTAINS Y'C'N ROLL RIGHT DOWN
IN CASE THERE'S A CHANGE IN THE WEATHER –

TWO BRIGHT SIDE-LIGHTS, WINKIN' AND BLINKIN',
AIN'T NO FINER RIG, I'M A-THINKIN'!
YOU C'N KEEP YER RIG IF YOU'RE THINKIN'
'AT I'D KEER TO SWAP
FER THAT SHINY LITTLE SURREY
WITH THE FRINGE ON THE TOP!

> (**LAUREY** *still pretends unconcern, but she is
> obviously slipping.*)

**AUNT ELLER.** *(Parlando.)*
WOULD Y'SAY THE FRINGE WAS MADE OF SILK?
**CURLY.**
WOULDN'T HAVE NO OTHER KIND OF SILK.
**LAUREY.** *(She's only human.)*
HAS IT REALLY GOT A TEAM OF SNOW-WHITE HORSES?
**CURLY.**
ONE'S LIKE SNOW – THE OTHER'S MORE LIKE MILK.
**AUNT ELLER.** So y'can tell 'em apart!

> (**CURLY** *and* **LAUREY** *cross back to the churn.*
> **LAUREY** *perches on it.* **CURLY** *puts his foot on
> the stool next to it.*)

**CURLY.**
ALL THE WORLD'LL FLY IN A FLURRY
WHEN I TAKE YOU OUT IN THE SURREY,
WHEN I TAKE YOU OUT IN THE SURREY
WITH THE FRINGE ON TOP!

WHEN WE HIT THAT ROAD, HELL FER LEATHER,
CATS AND DOGS'LL DANCE IN THE HEATHER,

BIRDS AND FROGS'LL SING ALL TOGETHER
AND THE TOADS WILL HOP!

THE WIND'LL WHISTLE AS WE RATTLE ALONG,
THE COWS'LL MOO IN THE CLOVER,
THE RIVER WILL RIPPLE OUT A WHISPERED SONG,
AND WHISPER IT OVER AND OVER:

> *(In a loud whisper.)*

DON'T YOU WISHT Y'D GO ON FEREVER?

> *(Almost involuntarily,* **AUNT ELLER** *joins him.)*

**CURLY & AUNT ELLER.**
DON'T YOU WISHT Y'D GO ON FEREVER?

> *(Likewise,* **LAUREY** *joins them both.)*

**LAUREY, CURLY & AUNT ELLER.**
DON'T YOU WISHT Y'D GO ON FEREVER
**CURLY.**
AND UD NEVER STOP
IN THAT SHINY LITTLE SURREY
WITH THE FRINGE ON THE TOP?

> *(Music continues under dialogue.)*

**AUNT ELLER.** Y'd shore feel like a queen settin' up in *that* carriage!

**CURLY.** *(Over-confident.)* On'y she talked so mean to me a while back, Aunt Eller, I'm a good mind not to take her.

**LAUREY.** Ain't said I was goin'!

**CURLY.** *(The fool.)* Ain't ast you!

**LAUREY.** Whur'd you git sich a rig at? *(With explosive laughter, seeing a chance for revenge.)* Anh! I bet he's went and h'ard a rig over to Claremore! Thinkin' I'd go with him!

**CURLY.** 'S all you know about it.

**LAUREY.** Spent all his money h'arin' a rig and now ain't got nobody to ride in it!

**CURLY.** Have, too! ...Did not h'ar it. Made the whole thing up outa my head.

**LAUREY.** What! Made it up?

**CURLY.** Dashboard and all.

**LAUREY.** *(Flying at him.)* Oh! Git offa the place, you! Aunt Eller, make him git his-se'f outa here.

> *(She picks up a carpet beater and chases* **CURLY.***)*

Tellin' me lies!

**CURLY.** *(Dodging her.)* Makin' up a few – look out now!

> *(He jumps the fence to save himself.* **LAUREY** *turns her back to him and sits down.* **CURLY** *comes up behind her. The music, which had become more turbulent to match the scene, now softens.)*

Makin' up a few purties ain't agin' no law 'at I know of. Don't you wisht they was sich a rig, though?

> *(Winking at* **AUNT ELLER.***)*

Nen y'could go to the play party and do a hoe-down till mornin' if you was a mind to...

> *(He gradually works his way down to the churn and sits on stool beside* **LAUREY.***)*

Nen when you was all wore out, I'd lift you onto the surrey, and jump up alongside of you – and we'd jist point the horses home... I can jist pitcher the whole thing.

> *(**AUNT ELLER** beams on them as* **CURLY** *sings very softly.)*

I CAN SEE THE STARS GITTIN' BLURRY
WHEN WE RIDE BACK HOME IN THE SURREY,
RIDIN' SLOWLY HOME IN THE SURREY
WITH THE FRINGE ON TOP.

I CAN FEEL THE DAY GITTIN' OLDER,
FEEL A SLEEPY HEAD NEAR MY SHOULDER,
NODDIN', DROOPIN' CLOSE TO MY SHOULDER
TILL IT FALLS, KERPLOP!

*(He places his hand on* **LAUREY**'s *cheek and nudges her head to his shoulder. As he continues singing, he smiles at* **AUNT ELLER,** *enjoying his success.)*

THE SUN IS SWIMMIN' ON THE RIM OF A HILL,
THE MOON IS TAKIN' A HEADER,
AND JIST AS I'M THINKIN' ALL THE EARTH IS STILL,
A LARK'LL WAKE UP IN THE MEDDER...

*(Parlando.)*

HUSH!

*(Sung.)*

YOU BIRD, MY BABY'S A-SLEEPIN' –
MAYBE GOT A DREAM WORTH A-KEEPIN'

*(Soothing and slower.)*

*(Parlando.)*

WHOA! YOU TEAM,

*(Sung.)*

AND JIST KEEP A-CREEPIN'
AT A SLOW CLIP-CLOP.
DON'T YOU HURRY WITH THE SURREY
WITH THE FRINGE ON THE TOP.

*(There is silence and contentment, but only for a brief moment.* **LAUREY** *starts slowly to emerge from the enchantment of his description.)*

**LAUREY.** On'y...on'y there ain't no sich rig. You said you made the whole thing up.

**CURLY.** Well...

**LAUREY.** *(Crossing to right,* **CURLY** *follows her.)* Why'd you come around here with yer stories and lies, gittin' me all worked up that-a-way? Talkin' 'bout the sun swimmin' on the hill, and all – like it was so. Who'd want to ride 'longside of you anyway?

*(***IKE** *and* **FRED** *enter and stand outside the gate, looking on.)*

**AUNT ELLER.** Whyn't you jist grab her and kiss her when she acts that-a-way, Curly? She's jist achin' fer you to, I bet.

**LAUREY.** Oh, I won't even speak to him, let alone 'low him to kiss me, the braggin', bow-legged, wisht-he-had-a-sweetheart bum!

> *(She flounces into the house, slamming the door.)*

**AUNT ELLER.** She likes you – quite a lot.

**CURLY.** Whew! If she liked me any more she'd sic the dogs onto me.

**IKE.** Y'git the wagon hitched up?

**AUNT ELLER.** Whut wagon?

**CURLY.** They's a crowd of folks comin' down from Bushyhead for the Box Social.

**FRED.** Curly said mebbe you'd loan us yer big wagon to bring 'em up from the station.

**AUNT ELLER.** Course I would, if he'd ast me.

**CURLY.** *(Embarrassed.)* Got to talkin' 'bout a lot of other things. I'll go hitch up the horses now 'f you say it's all right.

> *(As he exits through the gate and goes off left, a group of* **BOYS** *run on, leaping the fence, shouting boisterously and pushing* **WILL PARKER** *in front of them.* **WILL** *is apparently a favorite with* **AUNT ELLER.***)*

**SLIM.** See whut we brung you, Aunt Eller!

**AUNT ELLER.** Hi, Will!

**WILL.** Hi, Aunt Eller!

**AUNT ELLER.** Whut happened up at the fair? You do any good in the steer ropin'?

**WILL.** I did purty good. I won it.

**IKE.** Good boy!

**FRED.** Always knowed y'would.

**AUNT ELLER.** Ain't nobody c'n sling a rope like our territory boys.

**WILL.** Cain't stay but a minnit, Aunt Eller. Got to git over to Ado Annie. Don't you remember, her paw said 'f I ever was worth fifty dollars I could have her?

**AUNT ELLER.** Fifty dollars! That whut they give you fer prize money?

**WILL.** That's whut!

**AUNT ELLER.** Lands, if Ado Annie's paw keeps his promise we'll be dancin' at yer weddin'.

**WILL.** If he don't keep his promise I'll take her right from under his nose, and I won't give him the present I brung fer him.

*(He takes "The Little Wonder" from his pocket. This is a small, cylindrical toy with a peep-hole at one end.)*

Look, fellers, whut I got for Ado Annie's paw!

*(The **BOYS** crowd around.)*

'Scuse us, Aunt Eller.

*(Illustrating to the **BOYS**, lowering his voice.)*

You hold it up to yer eyes, like this. Then when you git a good look, you turn it around at th' top and the pitcher changes.

**IKE.** *(Looking into it.)* Well, I'll be side-gaited!

*(The **BOYS** line up and take turns, making appropriate exclamations.)*

**WILL.** They call it "The Little Wonder"!

**AUNT ELLER.** Silly goats!

*(But her curiosity gets the better of her. She yanks a **LITTLE MAN** out of the line, takes his place, gets hold of "The Little Wonder," and takes a look.)*

The hussy! ...Ought to be ashamed of herself.

*(Glaring at **WILL**.)*

You, too! How do you turn the thing to see the other pitcher?

(*Looking again, and turning.*)

**AUNT ELLER.** Wait, I'm gettin' it...

(*When she gets it, she takes it away from her eye quickly and, handing it to* **WILL**, *walks away in shocked silence. Then she suddenly "busts out laughin.'"*)

I'm a good mind to tell Ado Annie on yer.

**WILL.** Please don't, Aunt Eller. She wouldn't understand.

**AUNT ELLER.** No tellin' whut you been up to. Bet you carried on plenty in Kansas City.

**WILL.** I wouldn't call it carryin' on. But I shore did see some things I never see before.

### [MUSIC NO. 04 "KANSAS CITY"]

I GOT TO KANSAS CITY ON A FRID'Y.
BY SATTIDY I L'ARNED A THING OR TWO.
FOR UP TO THEN I DIDN'T HAVE AN IDY
OF WHUT THE MODREN WORLD WAS COMIN' TO!
I COUNTED TWENTY GAS BUGGIES GOIN' BY THEIRSEL'S
ALMOST EV'RY TIME I TUCK A WALK.
NEN I PUT MY EAR TO A BELL TELEPHONE
AND A STRANGE WOMERN STARTED IN TO TALK!

**AUNT ELLER.**

WHUT NEXT!

**BOYS.** (*Spoken.*)

YEAH, WHUT!

**WILL.**

WHUT NEXT?
EV'RYTHIN'S UP TO DATE IN KANSAS CITY.
THEY'VE GONE ABOUT AS FUR AS THEY C'N GO!
THEY WENT AND BUILT A SKYSCRAPER SEVEN STORIES HIGH –
ABOUT AS HIGH AS A BUILDIN' ORTA GROW.
EV'RYTHIN'S LIKE A DREAM IN KANSAS CITY.
IT'S BETTER THAN A MAGIC-LANTERN SHOW!
Y'C'N TURN THE RADIATOR ON WHENEVER YOU WANT
    SOME HEAT.

WITH EV'RY KIND O' COMFORT EV'RY HOUSE IS ALL
    COMPLETE.
YOU C'N WALK TO PRIVIES IN THE RAIN AN' NEVER WET
    YER FEET!
THEY'VE GONE ABOUT AS FUR AS THEY C'N GO!

**ALL.**

YES, SIR!
THEY'VE GONE ABOUT AS FUR AS THEY C'N GO!

**WILL.**

EV'RYTHIN'S UP TO DATE IN KANSAS CITY.
THEY'VE GONE ABOUT AS FUR AS THEY C'N GO!
THEY GOT A BIG THEAYTER THEY CALL A BURLEEKEW.
FER FIFTY CENTS YOU C'N SEE A DANDY SHOW.

**A BOY.** Girls?

**WILL.**

ONE OF THE GALS WAS FAT AND PINK AND PRETTY,
AS ROUND ABOVE AS SHE WAS ROUND BELOW.
I COULD SWEAR THAT SHE WAS PADDDED FROM HER
    SHOULDER
TO HER HEEL,
BUT LATER IN THE SECOND ACT WHEN SHE BEGAN TO
    PEEL
SHE PROVED THAT EV'RYTHIN' SHE HAD WAS
    ABSOLUTELY REAL!
SHE WENT ABOUT AS FUR AS SHE COULD GO!

**ALL.**

YES, SIR!
SHE WENT ABOUT AS FUR AS SHE COULD GO!

      (**WILL** *starts two-stepping.*)

**IKE.** Whut you doin', Will?

**WILL.** This is the two-step. That's all they're dancin'
nowadays. The waltz is through. Ketch on to it? A one
and a two – a one and a two. Course they don't do it
alone. C'mon, Aunt Eller.

      (**WILL** *dances* **AUNT ELLER** *around. At the end*
      *of the refrain she is all tuckered out.*)

**AUNT ELLER.**
　AND THAT'S ABOUT AS FUR AS I C'N GO!
**ALL.**
　YES, SIR!
　AND THAT'S ABOUT AS FUR AS SHE C'N GO!
　　　　(**WILL** *starts to dance alone.*)
**FRED.** Whut you doin' now, Will?
**WILL.** That's rag-time. Seen a couple of city fellers doin' it.
　　　　(*And* **WILL** *does his stuff, accompanied by four of the dancing* **BOYS.***)*
**ALL.**
　AND THAT'S ABOUT AS FUR AS HE C'N GO!
　　　　(*At end of number,* **CURLY** *enters.*)
**CURLY.** Team's all hitched.
**WILL.** 'Lo, Curly. Cain't stop to talk. Goin' over to Ado Annie's. I got fifty dollars.
**IKE.** Time we got goin', boys. Thanks fer the loan of the wagon, Aunt Eller.
　　　　(*They all start to leave.*)
　Come on, Curly.
**CURLY.** I'll ketch up with you.
　　　　(*He makes sure* **IKE** *is well on his way, then turns to* **AUNT ELLER.***)*
　Aunt Eller, I got to know sumpin'. Listen, who's the low, filthy sneak 'at Laurey's got her cap set for?
**AUNT ELLER.** You.
**CURLY.** Never mind 'at. They must be plenty of men a-tryin' to spark her. And she shorely leans to one of 'em. Now don't she?
**AUNT ELLER.** Well, they is that fine farmer, Jace Hutchins, jist this side of Lone Ellum – nen thet ole widder man at Claremore, makes out he's a doctor or a vet'nary –
　　　　(**JUD,** *a burly, scowling man, enters, carrying firewood.*)

**CURLY.** That's whut I thought. Hello, Jud.

**JUD.** Hello, yourself.

*(He exits into the house.)*

**AUNT ELLER.** *(Significantly, looking in* **JUD***'s direction.)* Nen of course there's someone nearer home that's got her on his mind most of the time, till he don't know a plow from a thrashin' machine.

**CURLY.** *(Jerking his head up toward the house.)* Him?

**AUNT ELLER.** Yeah, Jud Fry.

**CURLY.** That hardened, growly man?

**AUNT ELLER.** Now don't you go and say nuthin' agin' him! He's the best hired hand I ever had. Just about runs the farm by hisself. Well, two women couldn't do it, you orta know that.

**CURLY.** Laurey'd take up 'th a man like that?!

**AUNT ELLER.** I ain't said she's tuck up with him.

**CURLY.** Well, he's around all the time, ain't he? Lives here.

**AUNT ELLER.** Out in the smokehouse.

*(***JUD*** enters from the house, ***LAUREY*** following him. She lingers near the porch post while ***JUD*** crosses and speaks to ***AUNT ELLER***.)*

**JUD.** Changed my mind about cleanin' the henhouse today. Leavin' it till tomorrow. Got to quit early cuz I'm drivin' Laurey over to the party tonight.

*(A bombshell!)*

**CURLY.** You're drivin' Laurey?

**JUD.** Ast her.

*(Pointing to ***LAUREY***, who doesn't deny it. ***JUD*** exits. ***CURLY*** is completely deflated.)*

**CURLY.** Well, wouldn't that just make you bawl! Well, don't fergit, Aunt Eller. You and me's got a date together. And if you make up a nice box of lunch, mebbe I'll bid fer it.

**AUNT ELLER.** How we goin', Curly? In that rig you made up? I'll ride a-straddle of them lights a-winkin' like lightnin' bugs!

**CURLY.** That there ain't no made-up rig, you hear me? I h'ard it over to Claremore.

> *(This stuns* **LAUREY.***)*

**AUNT ELLER.** Lands, you did?

### [MUSIC NO. 05 "THE SURREY WITH THE FRINGE ON TOP (REPRISE)"]

**CURLY.** Shore did.

Purty one, too. When I come callin' fer you right after supper, see that you got yer beauty spots fastened onto you proper, so you won't lose 'em off, you hear? 'At's a right smart turnout.

> *(With false bravura, he picks up the refrain.)*

THE WHEELS ARE YELLER, THE UPHOLSTERY'S BROWN,
THE DASHBOARD'S GENUINE LEATHER,
WITH ISINGLASS CURTAINS Y'C'N ROLL RIGHT DOWN,
IN CASE THERE'S A CHANGE IN THE WEATHER –

> *(He breaks off in the song, turning to leave in the direction from which he entered.)*

See you before tonight anyways, on the way back from the station –

> *(Singing to himself as he saunters off.)*

AIN'T NO FINER RIG, I'M A-THINKIN'...
'AT I'D KEER TO SWAP
FER THAT SHINY LITTLE SURREY
WITH THE FRINGE ON THE TOP –

> *(He is off.)*

**AUNT ELLER.** *(Calling offstage to him.)* Hey, Curly, tell all the girls in Bushyhead to stop by here and freshen up. It's a long way to Skidmore's.

> *(Maybe* **LAUREY** *would like to "bust out" into tears, but she bites her lip and doesn't.* **AUNT ELLER** *studies her for a moment after* **CURLY** *has gone, then starts up toward the house.)*

That means we'll have a lot of company. Better pack yer lunch hamper.

**LAUREY.** *(A strange, sudden panic in her voice.)* Aunt Eller, don't go to Skidmore's with Curly tonight. If you do, I'll have to ride with Jud all alone.

**AUNT ELLER.** That's the way you wanted it, ain't it?

**LAUREY.** No. I did it because Curly was so fresh. But I'm afraid to tell Jud I won't go, Aunt Eller. He'd do sumpin turrble. He makes me shivver ever' time he gits clost to me... Ever go down to that ole smokehouse where he's at?

**AUNT ELLER.** Plen'y times. Why?

**LAUREY.** Did you see them pitchers he's got tacked onto the walls?

**AUNT ELLER.** Oh, yeah I seed them. But don't you pay them no mind.

**LAUREY.** Sumpin wrong inside him, Aunt Eller. I hook my door at night and fasten my winders agin' it. Agin' *it* – and the sound of feet a-walkin' up and down there under that tree outside my room.

**AUNT ELLER.** Laurey!

**LAUREY.** Mornin's he comes to his breakfast and looks at me out from under his eyebrows like sumpin back in the bresh som'eres. I know whut I'm talkin' about.

*(Voices offstage. It's **ADO ANNIE** and the **PEDDLER**.)*

**AUNT ELLER.** You crazy young 'un! Stop actin' like a chicken with its head cut off! Now who'd you reckon that is drove up? Why, it's that ole peddler! The one that sold me that egg-beater!

**LAUREY.** *(Looking off.)* He's got Ado Annie with him! Will Parker's Ado Annie!

**AUNT ELLER.** Ole peddler! You know whut he tol' me? Tol' me that egg-beater ud beat up eggs, and wring out dishrags, and turn the ice-cream freezer, and I don't know whut all!

**LAUREY.** *(Calling offstage.)* Yoohoo! Ado Annie!

**AUNT ELLER.** *(Shouting offstage.)* Hold yer horses, Peddler-man! I want to talk to you!

*(She starts off as* **ADO ANNIE** *enters with lunch hamper.)*

**ADO ANNIE.** Hi, Aunt Eller!

**AUNT ELLER.** Hi, yourself.

*(She exits.)*

**ADO ANNIE.** Hello, Laurey.

**LAUREY.** Hello. Will Parker's back from Kansas City. He's lookin' feryer.

*(* **ADO ANNIE***'s brows knit to meet a sudden problem.)*

**ADO ANNIE.** Will Parker! I didn't count on him bein' back so soon!

**LAUREY.** I can see that! Been ridin' a piece?

**ADO ANNIE.** The Peddler-man's gonna drive me to the Box Social. I got up sort of a tasty lunch.

**LAUREY.** Ado Annie! Have you tuck up with that Peddler-man?

**ADO ANNIE.** N-not yit.

**LAUREY.** But yer promised to Will Parker, ain't yer?

**ADO ANNIE.** Not what you might say *promised.* I jist told him mebbe.

**LAUREY.** Don't y' like him no more?

**ADO ANNIE.** Course I do. They won't never be nobody like Will.

**LAUREY.** Then whut about this Peddler-man?

**ADO ANNIE.** *(Looking off wistfully.)* They won't never be nobody like *him,* neither.

**LAUREY.** Well, which one d'you like the best?

**ADO ANNIE.** Whutever one I'm with!

**LAUREY.** Well, you air a silly!

**ADO ANNIE.** Now, Laurey, you know they didn't nobody pay me no mind up to this year, count of I was scrawny and flat as a beanpole. Nen I kind of rounded up a little and now the boys act diff'rent to me.

**LAUREY.** Well, whut's wrong with that?

**ADO ANNIE.** Nuthin' wrong. I like it. I like it so much when a feller talks purty to me I git all shaky from horn to hoof! Don't you?

**LAUREY.** Cain't think whut yer talkin' about.

**ADO ANNIE.** Don't you feel kind of sorry fer a feller when he looks like he wants to kiss ya?

**LAUREY.** Well, you jist cain't go around kissin' every man that asts you! Didn't anybody ever tell you that?

**ADO ANNIE.** Yeow, they *told* me...

## [MUSIC NO. 06 "I CAIN'T SAY NO"]

IT AIN'T SO MUCH A QUESTION OF NOT KNOWIN' WHUT
    TO DO,
I KNOWED WHUT'S RIGHT AND WRONG SINCE I BEEN TEN.
I HEARED A LOT OF STORIES – AND I RECKON THEY ARE
    TRUE –
ABOUT HOW GIRLS'RE PUT UPON BY MEN.
I KNOW I MUSTN'T FALL INTO THE PIT,
BUT WHEN I'M WITH A FELLER –

    *(Parlando.)*

I FERGIT!

    *(Sung.)*

I'M JIST A GIRL WHO CAIN'T SAY NO,
I'M IN A TURRIBLE FIX.
I ALWAYS SAY, "COME ON, LE'S GO!"
JIST WHEN I ORTA SAY NIX!

WHEN A PERSON TRIES TO KISS A GIRL
I KNOW SHE ORTA GIVE HIS FACE A SMACK.
BUT AS SOON AS SOMEONE KISSES ME
I SOMEHOW SORTA WANTA KISS HIM BACK!

I'M JIST A FOOL WHEN LIGHTS ARE LOW.
I CAIN'T BE PRISSY AND QUAINT –
I AIN'T THE TYPE THET C'N FAINT –
HOW C'N I BE WHUT I AIN'T?
I CAIN'T SAY NO!

WHUT YOU GOIN' TO DO WHEN A FELLER GITS FLIRTY
AND STARTS TO TALK PURTY?
WHUT YOU GOIN' TO DO?
S'POSIN' 'AT HE SAYS 'AT YER LIPS'RE LIKE CHERRIES,
ER ROSES, ER BERRIES?
WHUT YOU GOIN' TO DO?
S'POSIN' 'AT HE SAYS 'AT YOU'RE SWEETER'N CREAM
AND HE'S GOTTA HAVE CREAM ER DIE?
WHUT YOU GOIN' TO DO WHEN HE TALKS THET WAY?
SPIT IN HIS EYE?

I'M JIST A GIRL WHO CAIN'T SAY NO,
CAIN'T SEEM TO SAY IT AT ALL.
I HATE TO DISSERPOINT A BEAU
WHEN HE IS PAYIN' A CALL.
FER A WHILE I ACK REFINED AND COOL,
A-SETTIN' ON THE VELVETEEN SETTEE –
NEN I THINK OF THET OLE GOLDEN RULE,
AND DO FER HIM WHUT HE WOULD DO FER ME!

I CAIN'T RESIST A ROMEO
IN A SOMBRERO AND CHAPS.
SOON AS I SIT ON THEIR LAPS
SOMETHIN' INSIDE OF ME SNAPS –
I CAIN'T SAY NO!

*(She sits on her hamper and looks discouraged.)*
## [MUSIC NO. 07 "I CAIN'T SAY NO (ENCORE)"]

I'M JIST A GIRL WHO CAIN'T SAY NO.
KISSIN'S MY FAVORITE FOOD.
WITH ER WITHOUT THE MISTLETOE
I'M IN A HOLIDAY MOOD.

OTHER GIRLS ARE COY AND HARD TO CATCH,
BUT OTHER GIRLS AIN'T HAVIN' ANY FUN.
EV'RY TIME I LOSE A WRESTLIN' MATCH
I HAVE A FUNNY FEELIN' THAT I WON.

THOUGH I C'N FEEL THE UNDERTOW,
I NEVER MAKE A COMPLAINT
TILL IT'S TOO LATE FER RESTRAINT,
THEN WHEN I WANT TO I CAIN'T –
I CAIN'T SAY NO!

*(Resuming dialogue after applause.)*

It's like I tole you, I git sorry fer them!

**LAUREY.** I wouldn't feel sorry fer any man, no matter whut!

**ADO ANNIE.** I'm shore sorry fer pore Ali Hakim now. Look how Aunt Eller's cussin' him out!

**LAUREY.** Ali Hakim! That's his name?

**ADO ANNIE.** Yeah, it's Persian.

**LAUREY.** You shore fer sartin you love him better'n you love Will?

**ADO ANNIE.** I *was* shore. And now that ole Will has come home and first thing you know he'll start talkin' purty to me and changin' my mind back!

**LAUREY.** But Will wants to marry you.

**ADO ANNIE.** So does Ali Hakim.

**LAUREY.** Did he ast yer?

**ADO ANNIE.** Not direckly. But how I know is he said this mornin' that he wanted fer me to drive like that with him to the end of the world. Well, 'f we drove only as fur as Catoosie that'd take to sundown, wouldn't it? Nen, we'd have to go some'eres and be all night together, and bein' all night means he wants a weddin', don't it?

**LAUREY.** Not to a peddler it don't!

*(Enter **ALI HAKIM** and **AUNT ELLER**.)*

**ALI HAKIM.** All right! All right! If the egg-beater don't work I give you something just as good!

**AUNT ELLER.** Just as good! It's got to be a thousand million times better!

> *(**ALI** puts down his bulging suitcase. He rushes over and, to **LAUREY**'s alarm, kisses her hand.)*

**ALI HAKIM.** My, oh, my! Miss Laurey! Jippety crickets, how high you have growed up! Last time I come through here, you was tiny like a shrimp, with freckles. Now look at you – a great big beautiful lady!

**LAUREY.** Quit it a-bitin' me! If you ain't had no breakfast go and eat yerself a green apple.

**ALI HAKIM.** Now, Aunt Eller, just lissen –

**AUNT ELLER.** *(Shouting.)* I ain't yer Aunt Eller! Don't you call me Aunt Eller, you little wart. I'm mad at you.

**ALI HAKIM.** Don't you go and be mad at me. Ain't I said I'd give you a present?

> *(Getting his bag.)*

Something to wear.

**AUNT ELLER.** Foot! Got things fer to wear. Wouldn't have it. Whut is it?

**ALI HAKIM.** *(Holding up garter.)* Real silk. Made in Persia!

**AUNT ELLER.** Whut'd I want with a ole Persian garter?

**ADO ANNIE.** They look awful purty, Aunt Eller, with bows onto 'em and all.

**AUNT ELLER.** I'll try 'em on.

**ALI HAKIM.** Hold out your foot.

> *(**AUNT ELLER** obeys mechanically. But when **ALI** gets the garter over her ankle, she kicks him down.)*

**AUNT ELLER.** Did you have any idy I was goin' ter let you slide that garter up my limb?

> *(She stoops over and starts to pull the garter up.)*

Grab onto my petticoats, Laurey.

> *(Noticing **ALI** looking at her, she turns her back on him pointedly and goes on with the operation. **ALI** turns to **ADO ANNIE**.)*

**ALI HAKIM.** Funny woman. Would be much worse if I tried to take your garters off.

**ADO ANNIE.** Yeh, cuz that ud make her stockin's fall down, wouldn't it?

> *(A slow take, all three looking at **ADO ANNIE**.)*

**AUNT ELLER.** Now give me the other one.

**ALI HAKIM.** Which one?

*(Picking it out of his case.)*

Oh, you want to buy this one to match the other one?

**AUNT ELLER.** Whut do you mean do I want to *buy* it?

**ALI HAKIM.** I can let you have it for fifty cents – four bits.

**AUNT ELLER.** Do you want me to get that egg-beater and ram it down yer windpipe!

*(She snatches the second one away.)*

**ALI HAKIM.** All right – all right. Don't anybody want to buy something? How about you, Miss Laurey? Must be wanting something – a pretty young girl like you.

**LAUREY.** Me? Course I want sumpin. *(Working up to a kind of abstracted ecstasy.)* Want a buckle made outa shiny silver to fasten onto my shoes! Want a dress with lace. Want perfume, wanta be purty, wanta smell like a honeysuckle vine!

**AUNT ELLER.** Give her a cake of soap.

**LAUREY.** Want things I've heared of and never had before – a rubber-t'ard buggy, a cut-glass sugar bowl. Want things I cain't tell you about – not only to look at and hold in yer hands. Things to happen to you. Things so nice, if they ever did happen to you, yer heart ud quit beatin'. You'd fall down dead!

**ALI HAKIM.** I've got just the thing!

*(He fishes into his satchel and pulls out a bottle.)*

The Elixir of Egypt!

*(He holds the bottle high.)*

**LAUREY.** What's 'at?

**ALI HAKIM.** It's a secret formula, belonged to Pharaoh's daughter!

**AUNT ELLER.** *(Leaning over and putting her nose to it.)* Smellin' salts!

**ALI HAKIM.** *(Snatching it away.)* But a special kind of smelling salts. Read what it says on the label: "Take a deep breath and you see everything clear." That's what

Pharaoh's daughter used to do. When she had a hard problem to decide, like what prince she ought to marry, or what dress to wear to a party, or whether she ought to cut off somebody's head – she'd take a whiff of this.

**LAUREY.** *(Excited.)* I'll take a bottle of that, Mr. Peddler.

**ALI HAKIM.** Precious stuff.

**LAUREY.** How much?

**ALI HAKIM.** Two bits.

(**LAUREY** *pays him and takes the bottle.*)

**AUNT ELLER.** Throwin' away yer money!

**LAUREY.** *(Holding the bottle close to her, thinking aloud.)* Helps you decide what to do!

**ALI HAKIM.** Now don't you want me to show you some pretty dewdads? You know, with lace around the bottom, and ribbons running in and out?

**AUNT ELLER.** You mean fancy drawers?

**ALI HAKIM.** *(Taking a pair out of pack.)* All made in Paris.

**AUNT ELLER.** Well, I never wear that kind myself, but I shore do like to look at 'em.

(**ALI** *takes out a pair of red flannel drawers.*)

**ADO ANNIE.** *(Dubiously.)* Y-yeah, they's all right – if you ain't goin' no place.

**AUNT ELLER.** Bring yer trappin's inside and mebbe I c'n find you sumpin to eat and drink.

(*She exits.* **ALI** *starts to repack. The* **TWO GIRLS** *whisper for a moment.*)

**LAUREY.** Well, ast him, why don't you?

(*She giggles and exits into the house.*)

**ADO ANNIE.** Ali, Laurey and me've been havin' a argument.

**ALI HAKIM.** About what, baby?

**ADO ANNIE.** About what you meant when you said that about drivin' with me to the end of the world.

**ALI HAKIM.** *(Cagily.)* Well, I didn't mean really to the end of the world.

**ADO ANNIE.** Then how fur did you want to go?

**ALI HAKIM.** Oh, about as far as – say – Claremore – to the hotel.

**ADO ANNIE.** Whut's at the hotel?

**ALI HAKIM.** *(Ready for the kill.)* In front of the hotel is a veranda – inside is a lobby – upstairs – upstairs might be Paradise.

**ADO ANNIE.** I thought they was jist bedrooms.

**ALI HAKIM.** For you and me, baby – Paradise.

**ADO ANNIE.** Y'see! I knew I was right and Laurey was wrong! You do want to marry me, don't you?

**ALI HAKIM.** *(Embracing her impulsively.)* Ah, Ado Annie!

*(Pulling away.)*

What did you say?

**ADO ANNIE.** I said you do want to marry me, don't you. What *did you* say?

**ALI HAKIM.** I didn't say nothing!

**WILL.** *(Offstage.)* Whoa, Suzanna! Yoohoo, Ado Annie, I'm back!

**ADO ANNIE.** Oh, foot! Just when – 'lo, Will!

*(**WILL** lets out a whoop offstage.)*

That's Will Parker. Promise me you won't fight him.

**ALI HAKIM.** Why fight? I never saw the man before.

*(**WILL** enters.)*

**WILL.** Ado Annie! How's my honey-bunch? How's the sweetest little hundred-and-ten pounds of sugar in the territory?

**ADO ANNIE.** *(Confused.)* Er – Will, this is Ali Hakim.

**WILL.** How are yuh, Hak? Don't mind the way I talk. 'S all right. I'm goin' to marry her.

**ALI HAKIM.** *(Delighted.)* Marry her? On purpose?

**WILL.** Well, sure.

**ADO ANNIE.** No sich of a thing!

**ALI HAKIM.** It's a wonderful thing to be married.

*(He starts off.)*

**ADO ANNIE.** Ali!

**ALI HAKIM.** I got a brother in Persia, got six wives.

**ADO ANNIE.** Six wives? All at once?

**WILL.** Shore. 'At's a way they do in them countries.

**ALI HAKIM.** Not always. I got another brother in Persia only got one wife. He's a bachelor.

> *(Exit.)*

**ADO ANNIE.** Look, Will –

**WILL.** Look, Will, nuthin'. Know whut I got fer first prize at the fair? Fifty dollars!

**ADO ANNIE.** Well, that was good...

> *(The significance suddenly dawning on her.)*

Fifty dollars?

**WILL.** Ketch on? Yer paw promised I cud marry you 'f I cud git fifty dollars.

**ADO ANNIE.** 'At's right, he did.

**WILL.** Know whut I done with it? Spent it all on presents fer you!

**ADO ANNIE.** But if you spent it you ain't got the cash.

**WILL.** Whut I got is worth more'n the cash. Feller who sold me the stuff told me!

**ADO ANNIE.** But, Will...

**WILL.** Stop sayin' "But Will" – when do I git a little kiss? ... Oh, Ado Annie, honey, y'ain't been off my mind since I left. All the time at the fair grounds even, when I was chasin' steers.

> *(Mimicking the actions as he speaks them.)*

I'd rope one under the hoofs and pull him up sharp, and he'd land on his little rump...

> *(He looks lovingly at the imaginary steer's rump.)*

Nen I'd think of you.

**ADO ANNIE.** Don't start talkin' purty, Will.

**WILL.** See a lot of beautiful gals in Kansas City. Didn't give one a look.

**ADO ANNIE.** How could you see 'em if you didn't give 'em a look?

**WILL.** I mean I didn't look lovin' at 'em – like I look at you.

*(He turns and leans into her, slowly and deliberately, giving her an adoring and pathetic look.)*

**ADO ANNIE.** *(Backing away.)* Oh, Will, please don't look like that! I cain't bear it.

**WILL.** *(Advancing on her.)* Won't stop lookin' like this till you give me a little ole kiss.

**ADO ANNIE.** Oh, whut's a little ole kiss?

**WILL.** Nuthin' – less'n it comes from you.

*(Both stop.)*

**ADO ANNIE.** *(Sighing.)* You do talk purty!

**(WILL** *steps up for his kiss. She nearly gives in, but with sudden and unaccounted-for strength of character she turns away.)*

No, I won't!

### [MUSIC NO. 08 "ENTRANCE OF ENSEMBLE"]

**WILL.** *(Singing softly, seductively, "getting" her.)*
S'POSIN' 'AT I SAY 'AT YER LIPS'RE LIKE CHERRIES,
ER ROSES ER BERRIES?
WHUT YOU GONNA DO?

*(Putting her hand on his heart.)*

CAIN'T YOU FEEL MY HEART PALPATIN' AN' BUMPIN',
A-WAITIN' FER SUMPIN,
SUMPIN NICE FROM YOU?

I GOTTA GIT A KISS AN' IT'S GOTTA BE QUICK
ER I'LL JUMP IN A CRICK AN' DIE!

**ADO ANNIE.** *(Overcome.)*
WHUT'S A GIRL TO SAY WHEN YOU TALK THAT-A WAY?

*(They almost get to kiss, but on the downbeat of the next bar of music they are abruptly interrupted by a loud commotion offstage. The **BOYS** and **GIRLS** and **CURLY** and **GERTIE** enter with lunch hampers, shouting and laughing. **WILL** and **ADO ANNIE** run off. **AUNT ELLER** and **LAUREY** come out of the house. **GERTIE** laughs musically, an arpeggio up and down. **LAUREY**, unmindful of the group of girls she has been speaking to, looks across at **CURLY** and **GERTIE** and boils over. All the couples and **CURLY** and **GERTIE** waltz easily while they sing.)*

**ALL.**
OH, WHAT A BEAUTIFUL MORNIN',
**CURLY.**
OH, WHAT A BEAUTIFUL DAY.
**ALL.**
I GOT A BEAUTIFUL FEELIN'
**CURLY.**
EV'RYTHIN'S GOIN' MY WAY...

**AUNT ELLER.** *(To the rescue.)* Hey, Curly! Better take the wagon down to the troft and give the team some water.

**CURLY.** Right away, Aunt Eller.

*(He turns to go.)*

**GERTIE.** C'n I come, too? Just love to watch the way you handle horses.

**CURLY.** *(Looking across at **LAUREY**.)* 'At's about all I *can* handle, I reckon.

**GERTIE.** Oh, I cain't believe that, Curly – not from whut I heared about you!

*(She takes his arm and walks him off, turning on more musical laughter. A **GIRL** imitates her laugh. Crowd laughs. **LAUREY** takes an involuntary step forward, then stops, frustrated, furious.)*

**GIRL.** Looks like Curly's tuck up with that Cummin's girl.

**LAUREY.** Whut'd I keer about that?

> (*The* **GIRLS** *and* **LAUREY** *chatter and argue,
> ad-lib.*)

## [MUSIC NO. 09 "MANY A NEW DAY"]

**AUNT ELLER.** Come on, boys, better git these hampers out under the trees where it's cool.

> (*Exit* **AUNT ELLER** *and* **BOYS.** *To show "how
> little she keers,"* **LAUREY** *sings the following
> song.*)

**LAUREY.**

> WHY SHOULD A WOMERN WHO IS HEALTHY AND STRONG
> BLUBBER LIKE A BABY IF HER MAN GOES AWAY?
> A-WEEPIN' AND A-WAILIN' HOW HE'S DONE HER WRONG –
> THAT'S ONE THING YOU'LL NEVER HEAR ME SAY!
>
> NEVER GONNA THINK THAT THE MAN I LOSE
> IS THE ONLY MAN AMONG MEN.
> I'LL SNAP MY FINGERS TO SHOW I DON'T CARE.
> I'LL BUY ME A BRAND-NEW DRESS TO WEAR.
> I'LL SCRUB MY NECK AND I'LL BRESH MY HAIR,
> AND START ALL OVER AGAIN!
>
> MANY A NEW FACE WILL PLEASE MY EYE,
> MANY A NEW LOVE WILL FIND ME.
> NEVER'VE I ONCE LOOKED BACK TO SIGH
> OVER THE ROMANCE BEHIND ME.
> MANY A NEW DAY WILL DAWN BEFORE I DO!
>
> MANY A LIGHT LAD MAY KISS AND FLY,
> A KISS GONE BY IS BYGONE;
> NEVER'VE I ASKED AN AUGUST SKY,
> "WHERE HAS LAST JULY GONE?"
> NEVER'VE I WANDERED THROUGH THE RYE,
> WONDERIN' WHERE HAS SOME GUY GONE –
> MANY A NEW DAY WILL DAWN BEFORE I DO!

**GIRLS.**

> MANY A NEW FACE WILL PLEASE MY EYE,
> MANY A NEW LOVE WILL FIND ME.

NEVER'VE I ONCE LOOKED BACK TO SIGH
OVER THE ROMANCE BEHIND ME.
MANY A NEW DAY WILL DAWN BEFORE I DO!

**LAUREY.**

NEVER'VE I CHASED THE HONEY-BEE
WHO CARELESSLY CAJOLED ME.
SOMEBODY ELSE JUST AS SWEET AS HE
CHEERED ME AND CONSOLED ME.
NEVER'VE I WEPT INTO MY TEA
OVER THE DEAL SOMEONE DOLED ME.

**GIRLS.**

MANY A NEW DAY WILL DAWN,

**LAUREY.**

MANY A RED SUN WILL SET,
MANY A BLUE MOON WILL SHINE, BEFORE I DO!

*(A dance follows.)*

## [MUSIC NO. 10 "DANCE & MANY A NEW DAY (REPRISE)"]

**SINGING GIRLS.**

MANY A NEW FACE WILL PLEASE MY EYE,
MANY A NEW LOVE WILL FIND ME.
NEVER'VE I ONCE LOOKED BACK TO SIGH
OVER THE ROMANCE BEHIND ME.
MANY A NEW DAY WILL DAWN BEFORE I DO!

NEVER'VE I CHASED THE HONEY-BEE
WHO CARELESSLY CAJOLED ME.
SOMEBODY ELSE JUST AS SWEET AS HE
CHEERED ME AND CONSOLED ME.
NEVER'VE I WEPT INTO MY TEA
OVER THE DEAL SOMEONE DOLED ME.
MANY A NEW DAY WILL DAWN,

**LAUREY.**

MANY A RED SUN WILL SET,
MANY A BLUE MOON WILL SHINE, BEFORE I DO!

*(**LAUREY** and the **GIRLS** exit. When the stage is empty, **ALI** enters from the house, **ADO ANNIE***

*from the other side of the stage. He sees her and tries to duck back inside, but it's too late.)*

**ADO ANNIE.** Ali Hakim –

**ALI HAKIM.** Hello, kiddo.

**ADO ANNIE.** I'm shore sorry to see you so happy, cuz whut I got to say will make you mis'able... I got to marry Will.

**ALI HAKIM.** *(Faking despair.)* That's sad news for me. *(Noble.)* Well, he is a fine fellow.

**ADO ANNIE.** Don't hide your feelin's, Ali. I cain't stand it. I'd rather have you come right out and say yer heart is busted in two.

**ALI HAKIM.** Are you positive you got to marry Will?

**ADO ANNIE.** Shore's shootin'.

**ALI HAKIM.** And there is no chance for you to change your mind?

**ADO ANNIE.** No chance.

**ALI HAKIM.** *(As if granting a small favor.)* All right, then, my heart is busted in two.

**ADO ANNIE.** Oh, Ali, you do make up purty things to say!

**CARNES.** *(Offstage.)* That you, Annie?

**ADO ANNIE.** Hello, Paw.

> (**ANDREW CARNES** *enters. He is a scrappy man, carrying a shotgun.)*

Whut you been shootin'?

**CARNES.** Rabbits. That true whut I hear about Will Parker gittin' fifty dollars?

**ADO ANNIE.** That's right, Paw. And he wants to hold you to yer promise.

**CARNES.** Too bad. Still and all I cain't go back on my word.

**ADO ANNIE.** *(Glancing at **ALI HAKIM**.)* See, Ali!

**CARNES.** I advise you to git that money off 'n him before he loses it all. Put it in yer stockin' er inside yer corset where he cain't git at it...or can he?

**ADO ANNIE.** But, Paw – he ain't exackly kep' it. He spent it all on presents...

(**ALI** *is in a panic.*)

**CARNES.** See! Whut'd I tell you! Now he cain't have you. I said it had to be fifty dollars cash.

**ALI HAKIM.** But, Mr. Carnes, is that fair?

**CARNES.** Who the hell are you?

**ADO ANNIE.** This is Ali Hakim.

**CARNES.** Well, shet your face, er, I'll fill yer behind so full of buckshot, you'll be walkin' around like a duck the rest of yer life.

**ADO ANNIE.** Ali, if I don't have to marry Will, mebbe your heart don't have to be busted in two like you said.

**ALI HAKIM.** I did not say that.

**ADO ANNIE.** Oh, yes, you did.

**ALI HAKIM.** No, I did not.

**CARNES.** (*Brandishing his gun.*) Are you tryin' to make out my daughter to be a liar?

**ALI HAKIM.** No, I'm just making it clear what a liar I am if she's telling the truth.

**CARNES.** Whut else you been sayin' to my daughter?

**ADO ANNIE.** (*Before* **ALI** *can open his mouth.*) Oh, a awful lot.

**CARNES.** (*To* **ALI**.) When?

**ADO ANNIE.** Las' night, in the moonlight.

**CARNES.** (*To* **ALI**.) Where?

**ADO ANNIE.** 'Longside a haystack.

**ALI HAKIM.** Listen, Mr. Carnes...

**CARNES.** I'm lissening. Whut else did you say?

**ADO ANNIE.** He called me his Persian kitten.

**CARNES.** Why'd you call her that?

**ALI HAKIM.** I don't remember.

**ADO ANNIE.** I do. He said I was like a Persian kitten, cuz they was the cats with the soft round tails.

**CARNES.** (*Cocking his gun.*) That's enough. In this part of the country that better be a proposal of marriage.

**ADO ANNIE.** That's whut I thought.

**CARNES.** (*To* **ALI**.) Is that whut you think?

**ALI HAKIM.** Look, Mr. Carnes…

**CARNES.** *(Taking aim.)* I'm lookin'.

**ALI HAKIM.** I'm no good. I'm a peddler. A peddler travels up and down and all around

> *(Using **ADO ANNIE** as a buffer, he plants her between himself and **CARNES**.)*

and you'd hardly ever see your daughter no more.

> *(With his gun, **CARNES** nudges **ADO ANNIE** out of the way. She moves behind **ALI** to his right. **CARNES** lowers his gun and pats **ALI** on the back.)*

**CARNES.** That'd be all right. Take keer of her, son. Take keer of my little rosebud.

**ADO ANNIE.** Oh, Paw, that's purty.

> *(**CARNES** starts to exit into the house.)*

You shore fer sartin you can bear to let me go, Paw?

> *(**CARNES** turns.)*

**ALI HAKIM.** Are you *sure*, Mr. Carnes?

**CARNES.** *(Patting his gun.)* Just you try to change my mind.

> *(He takes a firmer grip on his gun and exits into the house.)*

**ADO ANNIE.** Oh, Ali Hakim, ain't it wonderful, Paw makin' up our mind fer us? He won't change neither. Onct he gives his word that you c'n have me, why, you *got* me.

**ALI HAKIM.** I *know* I got you.

**ADO ANNIE.** *(Starry-eyed.)* Mrs. Ali Hakim…the peddler's bride. Wait till I tell the girls.

> *(She exits. **ALI** leans against the porch post as the music starts.)*

## [MUSIC NO. 11 "IT'S A SCANDAL! IT'S A OUTRAGE!"]

> *(Then he starts to pace up and down, thinking hard, his head bowed, his hands behind his back. The orchestra starts a vamp that*

*continues under the melody. Some* **MEN** *enter and watch* **ALI** *curiously, but he is unmindful of them until they start to sing. Throughout his entire number,* **ALI** *must be burning, and he transmits his indignation to the* **MEN** *who sing in a spirit of angry protest by the time the refrain is reached.)*

**ALI HAKIM.** *(Spoken in rhythm. Circling the stage.)*
TRAPPED! ...
TRICKED! ...
HOODBLINKED! ...
HAMBUSHED! ...

**MEN.**
FRIEND,
WHUT'S ON YER MIND?
WHY DO YOU WALK
AROUND AND AROUND,
WITH YER HANDS
FOLDED BEHIND,
AND YER CHIN
SCRAPIN' THE GROUND?

> **(ALI** *walks away, then comes back to them and starts to pour out his heart.)*

**ALI HAKIM.** *(Spoken freely.)*
TWENTY MINUTES AGO I AM FREE LIKE A BREEZE,
FREE LIKE A BIRD IN THE WOODLAND WILD,
FREE LIKE A GYPSY,* FREE LIKE A CHILD,
I'M UNATTACHED!

TWENTY MINUTES AGO I CAN DO WHAT I PLEASE,
FLICK MY CIGAR ASHES ON A RUG,
DUNK WITH A DOUGHNUT, DRINK FROM A JUG –
I'M A HAPPY MAN!
*(Crescendo.)*

I'M MINDING MY OWN BUSINESS LIKE I OUGHTER,
AIN'T MEANING ANY HARM TO ANYONE.

---

*All instances of "gypsy" can be changed if necessary for your production. Please submit a dialogue change request to your licensing representative.

I'M TALKING TO A CERTAIN FARMER'S DAUGHTER –
THEN – I'M LOOKING IN THE MUZZLE OF A GUN!

**MEN.**

IT'S GITTIN' SO YOU CAIN'T HAVE ANY FUN!
EV'RY DAUGHTER HAS A FATHER WITH A GUN!

IT'S A SCANDAL, IT'S A OUTRAGE!
HOW A GAL GITS A HUSBAND TODAY!

**ALI HAKIM.**

IF YOU MAKE ONE MISTAKE WHEN THE MOON IS BRIGHT,
THEN THEY TIE YOU TO A CONTRACT, SO YOU MAKE IT
EV'RY NIGHT!

**MEN.**

IT'S A SCANDAL, IT'S A OUTRAGE!
WHEN HER FAMBLY SURROUND YOU AND SAY:
"YOU GOTTA TAKE AN' MAKE AN HONEST WOMERN OUTA
NELL!"

**ALI HAKIM.**

TO MAKE YOU MAKE HER HONEST, SHE WILL LIE LIKE
HELL!

**MEN.**

IT'S A SCANDAL, IT'S A OUTRAGE!
ON OUR MANHOOD, IT'S A BLOT!
WHERE IS THE LEADER WHO WILL SAVE US?
AND BE THE FIRST MAN TO BE SHOT?

**ALI HAKIM.** Me?

**MEN.** Yes, you!

IT'S A SCANDAL, IT'S A OUTRAGE!
JIST A WINK AND A KISS AND YOU'RE THROUGH!

**ALI HAKIM.**

YOU'RE A MESS, AND IN LESS THAN A YEAR, BY HECK!
THERE'S A BABY ON YOUR SHOULDER MAKING BUBBLES
ON YOUR NECK!

(**ADO ANNIE** *and some of the* **GIRLS** *filter on
from stage right.*)

**MEN.**

IT'S A SCANDAL, IT'S A OUTRAGE!
ANY FARMER WILL TELL YOU IT'S TRUE.

**ALI HAKIM.**

A ROOSTER IN A CHICKEN COOP IS BETTER OFF'N MEN.
HE AIN'T THE SPECIAL PROPERTY OF JUST ONE HEN!

**MEN.**

IT'S A SCANDAL, IT'S A OUTRAGE!
IT'S A PROBLEM WE MUST SOLVE!
WE GOTTA START A REVOLUTION!

**GIRLS.**

ALL RIGHT, BOYS! REVOLVE!

(*The* **BOYS** *swing around, see the* **GIRLS** *and are immediately cowed. Several of the* **GIRLS** *go after their* **MEN**, *capturing them and dragging them off in various ways. Four of the* **MEN** *lift* **ALI** *over their heads and carry him off. As the music ends,* **GERTIE** *enters through the gate with* **CURLY** *as* **LAUREY** *enters on the porch and starts packing her lunch hamper.*)

**GERTIE.** Hello, Laurey. Just packin' yer hamper now?

**LAUREY.** I been busy.

(**GERTIE** *looks in* **LAUREY**'*s hamper.* **AUNT ELLER** *enters.*)

**GERTIE.** You got gooseberry tarts, too. Wonder if they is as light as mine. Mine'd like to float away if you blew on them.

**LAUREY.** I did blow on one of mine and it broke up into a million pieces.

(**GERTIE** *laughs – that laugh again.*)

**GERTIE.** Ain't she funny!

(*The* **GIRLS** *step toward each other menacingly.*)

**AUNT ELLER.** Gertie! Better come inside, and cool off.

**GERTIE.** You comin' inside with me, Curly?

**CURLY.** Not jist yet.

**GERTIE.** Well, don't be too long. And don't fergit when the auction starts tonight, mine's the biggest hamper.

(*The laugh again, and she exits into the house.*)

LAUREY. *(Going on with her packing.)* So that's the Cummin's girl I heard so much talk of.

CURLY. You seen her before, ain't you?

LAUREY. Yeow. But not since she got so old. Never did see anybody get so peeked-lookin' in sich a short time.

AUNT ELLER. *(Amused at* LAUREY.*)* Yeah, and she says she's only eighteen. I betcha she's nineteen.

> *(She exits into the house.)*

CURLY. What ya got in yer hamper?

LAUREY. 'At's jist some ole meat pies and apple jelly. Nuthin' like whut Gertie Cummin's has in *her* basket.

> *(She sits on the arm of a rocking chair.)*

CURLY. You really goin' to drive to the Box Social with that Jud feller?

> *(Pause.)*

LAUREY. Reckon so. Why?

CURLY. Nuthin'... It's jist that ev'rybody seems to expec' *me* to take you.

> *(He sits on the other arm of the rocker.)*

LAUREY. Then, mebbe it's jist as well you ain't. We don't want people talkin' 'bout us, do we?

CURLY. You think people *do* talk about us?

LAUREY. Oh, you know how they air – like a swarm of mudwasps. Alw'ys gotta be buzzin' 'bout sumpin.

CURLY. *(Rocking the chair.)* Well, whut're they sayin'? That you're stuck on me?

LAUREY. No. Most of the talk is that you're stuck on me.

## [MUSIC NO. 12 "PEOPLE WILL SAY WE'RE IN LOVE"]

CURLY. Cain't imagine how these ugly rumors start.

LAUREY. Me neither.

> WHY DO THEY THINK UP STORIES THAT LINK
> MY NAME WITH YOURS?

**CURLY.**

> WHY DO THE NEIGHBORS GOSSIP ALL DAY
> BEHIND THEIR DOORS?

**LAUREY.**

> I KNOW A WAY TO PROVE WHAT THEY SAY
> IS QUITE UNTRUE;
> HERE IS THE GIST, A PRACTICAL LIST
> OF "DON'TS" FOR YOU:
>
> DON'T THROW BOUQUETS AT ME –
> DON'T PLEASE MY FOLKS TOO MUCH,
> DON'T LAUGH AT MY JOKES TOO MUCH –
> PEOPLE WILL SAY WE'RE IN LOVE!

**CURLY.** *(Leaving her.)* Who laughs at yer jokes?

**LAUREY.** *(Following him.)*

> DON'T SIGH AND GAZE AT ME,
> (YOUR SIGHS ARE SO LIKE MINE,)

> > **(CURLY** *turns to embrace her, she stops him.)*

> YOUR EYES MUSTN'T GLOW LIKE MINE –
> PEOPLE WILL SAY WE'RE IN LOVE!
> DON'T START COLLECTING THINGS –

**CURLY.** Like whut?

**LAUREY.**

> GIVE ME MY ROSE AND MY GLOVE.

> > **(CURLY** *looks away, guiltily.)*

> SWEETHEART, THEY'RE SUSPECTING THINGS –
> PEOPLE WILL SAY WE'RE IN LOVE!

**CURLY.**

> SOME PEOPLE CLAIM THAT YOU ARE TO BLAME
> AS MUCH AS I –

> > **(LAUREY** *is about to deny this.)*

> WHY DO YOU TAKE THE TROUBLE TO BAKE
> MY FAV'RITE PIE?

> > *(Now* **LAUREY** *looks guiltily.)*

> GRANTIN' YOUR WISH, I CARVED OUR INITIALS ON THAT
>    TREE...

*(He points off at the tree.)*

JIST KEEP A SLICE OF ALL THE ADVICE
YOU GIVE, SO FREE!

DON'T PRAISE MY CHARM TOO MUCH,
DON'T LOOK SO VAIN WITH ME,
DON'T STAND IN THE RAIN WITH ME –
PEOPLE WILL SAY WE'RE IN LOVE!

DON'T TAKE MY ARM TOO MUCH,
DON'T KEEP YOUR HAND IN MINE,
YOUR HAND FEELS SO GRAND IN MINE,
PEOPLE WILL SAY WE'RE IN LOVE!

DON'T DANCE ALL NIGHT WITH ME,
TILL THE STARS FADE FROM ABOVE.
THEY'LL SEE IT'S ALL RIGHT WITH ME,
PEOPLE WILL SAY WE'RE IN LOVE!

*(Music continues as **CURLY** speaks.)*

Don't you reckon y'could tell Jud you'd rather go with me tonight?

**LAUREY.** Curly! I – no, I couldn't.

**CURLY.** Oh, you couldn't?
*(Frowning.)* Think I'll go down to the smokehouse, where Jud's at. See whut's so elegant about him, makes girls wanta go to parties with him.

*(He starts off, angrily.)*

**LAUREY.** Curly!

**CURLY.** *(Turning.)* Whut?

**LAUREY.** Nuthin'.

*(She watches **CURLY** as he exits, then sits on the rocker, crying softly, and starts to sing.)*

DON'T SIGH AND GAZE AT ME,
(YOUR SIGHS ARE SO LIKE MINE,)
YOUR EYES MUSTN'T GLOW LIKE MINE –

*(Music continues. She chokes up, can't go on.
**AUNT ELLER** has come out and looks with great
understanding.)*

**AUNT ELLER.** Got yer hamper packed?

**LAUREY.** *(Snapping out of it.)* Oh, Aunt Eller... Yes, nearly.

**AUNT ELLER.** Like a hanky?

**LAUREY.** Whut'd I want with a ole hanky?

**AUNT ELLER.** Y'got a smudge on yer cheek – jist under yer eye.

> *(**LAUREY** dries her eyes, starts toward the house, thinks about the bottle of "Elixir of Egypt," picks it up, looks at **AUNT ELLER**, and runs out through the gate and offstage. **AUNT ELLER** sits in the rocker and hums the refrain, happy and contented, as the lights dim.)*

**[MUSIC NO. 13 "CHANGE OF SCENE"]**

## Scene Two
## The Smokehouse

*(The smokehouse. Immediately after Scene One. It is a dark, dirty building where the meat was once kept. The rafters are smoky, covered with dust and cobwebs. On a low loft many things are stored – horse collars, plowshares, a binder twine, a keg of nails. Under it, the bed is grimy and never made. On the walls, tobacco advertisements and pink covers of* Police Gazettes. *In a corner there are hoes, rakes, and an axe. Two chairs, a table, and a spittoon comprise the furniture. There is a mirror for shaving, several farm lanterns, and a rope. A small window lets in a little light, but not much.)*

*(**JUD** enters and crosses to the table. There is a knock on the door. **JUD** rises quickly and tiptoes to the window to peek outside. Then he glides swiftly back to the table. Takes out a pistol and starts to polish it. There is a second knock.)*

**JUD.** *(Calling out sullenly.)* Well, open it, cain't you?

**CURLY.** *(Opening the door and strolling in.)* Howdy.

**JUD.** Whut'd you want?

**CURLY.** I done got th'ough my business up here at the house. Just thought I'd pay a call.

*(Pause.)*

You got a gun, I see.

**JUD.** Good un. Colt forty-five.

**CURLY.** Whut do you do with it?

**JUD.** Shoot things.

**CURLY.** Oh.

*(He moseys around the room casually.)*

**CURLY**. That there pink picture – now that's a naked womern, ain't it?

**JUD**. Yer eyes don't lie to you.

**CURLY**. Plumb stark naked as a jaybird. No. No, she ain't. Not quite. Got a couple of thingam'bobs tied onto her.

**JUD**. Shucks. That ain't a thing to whut I got here.

> *(He shoves a pack of postcards across the table toward* **CURLY**.*)*

Lookit that top one.

**CURLY**. *(Covering his eyes.)* I'll go blind! ...

> *(Tosses it back on the table.)*

That ud give me idys, that would.

**JUD**. *(Picking it up and looking at it.)* That's a dinger, that is.

**CURLY**. *(Gravely.)* Yeah, that shore is a dinger...

> *(Taking down a rope.)*

That's a good-lookin' rope you got there.

> *(He begins to spin it.)*

Spins nice. You know Will Parker? He can shore spin a rope.

> *(He tosses one end of the rope over the rafter and pulls down on both ends, tentatively.)*

'S a good strong hook you got there. You could hang yerself on that, Jud.

**JUD**. I could whut?

**CURLY**. *(Cheerfully.)* Hang yerself. It ud be as easy as fallin' off a log! Fact is, you could stand on a log – er a cheer if you'd rather – right about here – see? And put this here around yer neck. Tie that good up there first, of course. Then all you'd have to do would be to fall off the log – er the cheer, whichever you'd ruther fall off of. In five minutes, or less, with good luck, you'd be daid as a doornail.

**JUD**. Whut'd you mean by that?

**CURLY.** Nen folks ud come to yer funril and sing sad songs.

**JUD.** *(Disdainfully.)* Yamnh!

**CURLY.** They would. You never know how many people like you till yer daid.

> *(As he speaks the next line, he defines the space where the "coffin" lies.)*

Y'd prob'ly be laid out in the parlor.

> *(Gesturing over "Jud's body" as he speaks.)*

Y'd be all diked out in yer best suit with yer hair combed down slick, and a high starched collar.

**JUD.** *(Beginning to visualize the "scene"* **CURLY** *is setting.)* Would they be any flowers, d'you think?

**CURLY.** Shore would, and palms, too – all around yer cawfin. Nen folks ud stand around you and the men ud bare their heads and the womern would sniffle softly. Some'd prob'ly faint – ones that tuck a shine to you when you wuz alive.

**JUD.** Whut womern ever tuck a shine to me?

**CURLY.** Lots of womern. On'y they don't never come right out and show you how they feel –

> *(Again indicating the "coffin.")*

less'n you die first.

**JUD.** *(Thoughtfully.)* I guess that's so.

**CURLY.** They'd shore sing loud though when the singin' started – sing like their hearts ud break!

### [MUSIC NO. 14 "PORE JUD IS DAID"]

> *(He starts to sing very earnestly and solemnly, improvising the sort of thing he thinks might be sung.)*

PORE JUD IS DAID,
PORE JUD FRY IS DAID!
ALL GETHER ROUND HIS CAWFIN NOW AND CRY.
HE HAD A HEART OF GOLD
AND HE WASN'T VERY OLD –
OH, WHY DID SICH A FELLER HAVE TO DIE?

*(During the following, JUD slowly stands, next to but not too close to CURLY, mesmerized by the imaginary body laid out in front of them.)*

PORE JUD IS DAID,
PORE JUD FRY IS DAID!
HE'S LOOKIN', OH, SO PEACEFUL AND SERENE.

**JUD.** *(Touched and suddenly carried away, he sings a soft response.)*

AND SERENE!

*(Takes off hat.)*

**CURLY.**

HE'S ALL LAID OUT TO REST
WITH HIS HANDS ACROST HIS CHEST.
HIS FINGERNAILS HAVE NEVER B'EN SO CLEAN!

*(JUD turns slowly to question the good taste of this last reference, but CURLY plunges straight into another item of the imagined wake.)*

Nen the preacher'd git up and he'd say:

*(Chanting.)* "Folks! We are gethered here to moan and groan over our brother Jud Fry who hung hisse'f up by a rope in the smokehouse."

*(Speaking.)* Nen there'd be weepin' and wailin' *(Significantly.)* from some of those womern.

*(JUD nods his head understandingly.)*

Nen he'd say, *(Chanting.)* "Jud was the most misunderstood man in the territory. People useter think he was a mean, ugly feller.

*(JUD looks up.)*

"And they called him a dirty skunk and a ornery pig-stealer.

*(CURLY switches quickly; he sings.)*

"BUT – THE FOLKS 'AT REALLY KNOWED HIM,
KNOWED 'AT BENEATH THEM TWO DIRTY SHIRTS HE
     ALW'YS WORE,
THERE BEAT A HEART AS BIG AS ALL OUTDOORS."

**JUD.** *(Repeating reverently like someone at a revivalist meeting.)*

AS BIG AS ALL OUTDOORS.

**CURLY.**

JUD FRY LOVED HIS FELLOW MAN.

**JUD.**

HE LOVED HIS FELLOW MAN.

> *(**CURLY** is warming up and speaks with the impassioned inflections of an Evangelist.)*

**CURLY.** He loved the birds of the forest and the beasts of the field. He loved the mice and the vermin in the barn, and he treated the rats like equals – which was right. And he loved little children. He loved ev'body and ev'thin' in the world! ...Only he never let on, so nobody ever knowed it!

> *(Returning to vigorous song.)*

PORE JUD IS DAID,

PORE JUD FRY IS DAID!

HIS FRIENDS'LL WEEP AND WAIL FER MILES AROUND.

**JUD.** *(Now right into it.)*

MILES AROUND.

**CURLY.**

THE DAISIES IN THE DELL

WILL GIVE OUT A DIFF'RUNT SMELL

BECUZ PORE JUD IS UNDERNEATH THE GROUND.

> *(**JUD** is too emotionally exalted by the spirit of **CURLY**'s singing to be analytical. He now takes up a refrain of his own.)*

**JUD.**

PORE JUD IS DAID,

A CANDLE LIGHTS HIS HAID,

HE'S LAYIN' IN A CAWFIN MADE OF WOOD –

**CURLY.**

WOOD.

**JUD.**

AND FOLKS ARE FEELIN' SAD

CUZ THEY USETER TREAT HIM BAD,

AND NOW THEY KNOW THEIR FRIEND HAS GONE FER
GOOD –

**CURLY.** *(Softly.)*

GOOD.

**JUD & CURLY.**

PORE JUD IS DAID,
A CANDLE LIGHTS HIS HAID!

**CURLY.**

HE'S LOOKIN', OH, SO PURTY AND SO NICE.
HE LOOKS LIKE HE'S ASLEEP.
IT'S A SHAME THAT HE WON'T KEEP,
BUT IT'S SUMMER AND WE'RE RUNNIN' OUT OF ICE...

**JUD & CURLY.** *(Singing in harmony.)*

PORE JUD!
PORE JUD!

> (**JUD** *breaks down, weeps, and sits at the table,
> burying his head in his arms.*)

**CURLY.** Yes, sir. That's the way it ud be. Shore be an interstin' funril. Wouldn't like to miss it.

**JUD.** *(His eyes narrowing.)* Wouldn't like to miss it, eh? Well, mebbe you will.

> (*He resumes polishing the gun.*)

Mebbe you'll go first.

**CURLY.** *(Sitting down.)* Mebbe... Le's see now, whur did you work at before you come here? Up by Quapaw, wasn't it?

**JUD.** Yeah, and before that over by Tulsa. Lousy they was to me. Both of 'em. Always makin' out they was better. Treatin' me like dirt.

**CURLY.** And whut'd you do – git even?

**JUD.** Who said anythin' about gittin' even?

**CURLY.** No one, that I recollect. It jist come into my head.

**JUD.** If it ever come to gittin' even with anybody, I'd know how to do it.

**CURLY.** *(Looking down at gun and pointing.)* That?

**JUD.** Nanh! They's safer ways then that, if you use yer brains... 'Member that far on the Bartlett farm over by Sweetwater?

**CURLY.** Shore do. 'Bout five years ago. Turrble accident. Burned up the father, and mother and daughter.

**JUD.** That warn't no accident. A feller told me – the h'ard hand was stuck on the Bartlett girl, and he found her in the hayloft with another feller.

**CURLY.** And it was him that burned the place?

**JUD.** *(Nodding.)* It tuck him weeks to git all the kerosene – buying it at different times – feller who told me made out it happened in Missouri, but I knowed all the time it was the Bartlett farm. Whut a liar he was!

**CURLY.** A kind of a murderer, too. Wasn't he?

> *(He rises, goes over to the door, and opens it.)*

Git a little air in here.

**JUD.** You ain't told me yet whut business you had here. We got no cattle to sell ner no cow ponies. The oat crop is done spoke fer.

**CURLY.** You shore relieved my mind consid'able.

**JUD.** *(Tensely.)* They's on'y one other thing on this farm you could want – and it better not be that!

**CURLY.** *(Closing the door deliberately and turning slowly to face* **JUD.***)* But that's jist whut it is.

**JUD.** Better not be! You keep away from her, you hear?

**CURLY.** *(Coolly.)* You know somebody orta tell Laurey whut kind of a man you air. And fer that matter, somebody orta tell *you* onct about yerself.

**JUD.** You better git outa here, Curly.

**CURLY.** A feller wouldn't feel very safe in here with you... 'f he didn't know you.
*(Acidly.)* But I know you, Jud.

> *(He looks* **JUD** *straight in the eye. As he continues, he crosses upstage behind* **JUD,** *slowly closing in on him.)*

CURLY. In this country, they's two things you c'n do if you're a man. Live out of doors is one. Live in a hole is the other. I've set by my horse in the bresh som'eres and heared a rattlesnake many a time. Rattle, rattle, rattle! – he'd go, skeered to death. Somebody comin' close to his hole! Somebody gonna step on him! Git his old fangs ready, full of pizen! Curl up and wait! – Long's you live in a hole, you're skeered, you got to have perfection. You c'n have muscles, oh, like arn – and still be as weak as a empty bladder – less'n you got things to barb yer hide with.

*(Suddenly, harshly, directly to* JUD.*)* How'd you git to be the way you air, anyway – settin' here in this filthy hole – and thinkin' the way you're thinkin'? Why don't you do sumpin healthy onct in a while, 'stid of stayin' shet up here – a-crawlin' and festerin'!

> *(*JUD*'s polishing of his gun has turned into a kind of desperate frenzy. In a reflex action, he raises his arm and the gun goes off.)*

JUD. Anh!

> *(Luckily the gun is pointed toward the ceiling.)*

CURLY. *(Reacting to the shot, he draws his own gun.)* You orta feel better now. Hard on the roof, though. I wisht you'd let me show you sumpin.

> *(*JUD *doesn't move, but stands staring into* CURLY*'s eyes.)*

They's a knot-hole over there about as big as a dime. See it a-winkin'? I jist want to see if I c'n hit it.

> *(Unhurriedly, with cat-like tension, he turns and fires high up at the wall.)*

Bullet right through the knot-hole, 'thout tetchin', slick as a whistle, didn't I? I knowed I could do it. You saw it, too, didn't you?

> *(Ad-lib offstage.)*

Somebody's a-comin', I 'spect.

(**CURLY** *and* **JUD** *assume casual positions.*
**AUNT ELLER**, **ALI HAKIM**, *and several others
come running in.*)

**AUNT ELLER.** *(Gasping for breath.)* Who f'ard off a gun? Was
that you, Curly? Don't set there, you lummy. Answer
when you're spoke to?

**CURLY.** Well, I shot onct.

**AUNT ELLER.** What was you shootin' at?

**CURLY.** *(Rises.)* See that knot-hole over there?

**AUNT ELLER.** I see lots of knot-holes.

**CURLY.** Well, it was one of them.

**AUNT ELLER.** *(Exasperated.)* Well, ain't you a pair of purty
nuthin's, a-pickin' away at knot-holes and skeerin'
everybody to death! Orta give you a good Dutch rub
and arn some of the craziness out of you!
*(Calling off to people in doorway.)* 'S all right! Nobody
hurt. Just a pair of fools swappin' noises.

*(She exits.)*

**ALI HAKIM.** *(Appearing in the doorway.)* Mind if I visit with
you, gents? It's good to get away from the women for
a while. Now then, we're all by ourselves. I got a few
purties, private knickknacks for to show you. Special
for the menfolks.

*(He starts to get them out.)*

**CURLY.** See you gentlemen later. I gotta git a surrey I h'ard
fer tonight.

*(He starts to go.)*

**ALI HAKIM.** *(Shoving cards under* **JUD**'s *nose.)* Art postcards.

**JUD.** *(To* **CURLY**.*)* Who you think yer takin' in that surrey?

**CURLY.** Aunt Eller – and Laurey, if she'll come with me.

**JUD.** She won't.

**CURLY.** Mebbe she will.

*(He exits.)*

**JUD.** *(Raising his voice after* **CURLY.***)* She promised to go with me, and she better not change her mind. She better not!

**ALI HAKIM.** Now, I want you to look at these straight from Paris.

**JUD.** I don't want none o' them things now. Got any frog stickers?

**ALI HAKIM.** You mean one of them long knives? What would you want with a thing like that?

**JUD.** I dunno. Kill a hog – er a skunk. It's all the same, ain't it? I tell you whut I'd like better'n a frog sticker, if you got one. Ever hear of one of them things you call "The Little Wonder"? It's a thing you hold up to your eyes to see pitchers, only that ain't all they is to it...not quite. Y'see it's got a little jigger onto it, and you tetch it and out springs a sharp blade.

**ALI HAKIM.** On a spring, eh?

**JUD.** Y'say to a feller, "Look through this." Nen when he's looking you snap out the blade. It's jist above his chest and, bang! Down you come.

> *(Slaps* **ALI** *on the chest, knocking the wind from him.)*

**ALI HAKIM.** *(He recovers from the blow, but* **JUD** *is beginning to make him nervous.)* A good joke to play on a friend... I – er – don't handle things like that. Too dangerous. What I'd like to show you is my new stock of postcards.

**JUD.** Don't want none. Sick of them things. I'm going to get me a real womern.

**ALI HAKIM.** What would you want with a woman? Why, I'm having trouble right now, all on account of a woman. And you say you *want* one. Why? Look at you! You're a man who is free to come and go as you please. You got a nice cozy little place.

> *(Looking the place over.)*

Private. Nobody to bother you. Artistic pictures. They don't talk back to you...

**JUD.** I'm t'ard of all these *pitchers* of womern!

**ALI HAKIM.** All right. You're tired of them. So throw 'em away and buy some new ones.

*(Showing* **JUD** *cards again.)*

You get tired of a woman and what can you do? Nothing! Just keep getting tireder and tireder!

**JUD.** I made up my mind.

**ALI HAKIM.** *(He packs his bag and starts off. Suddenly, a light bulb goes off in his head, and he pauses.)* So...
*(Back to* **JUD.**) you want a real woman? Say, do you happen to know a girl named Ado Annie?

**JUD.** I don't want her.

**ALI HAKIM.** I don't want her either. But I got her!

*(He exits.)*

**JUD.** Don't want nuthin' from no peddler. Want real things! Whut am I doin' shet up here – like that feller says – a-crawlin' and a-festerin'? Whut am I doin' in this lousy smokehouse?

### [MUSIC NO. 15 "LONELY ROOM"]

*(He sits and looks about the room, scowling. Then he starts to sing, half-talking at first, then singing in full voice.)*

THE FLOOR CREAKS,
THE DOOR SQUEAKS,
THERE'S A FIELD MOUSE A-NIBBLIN' ON A BROOM,
AND I SET BY MYSELF
LIKE A COBWEB ON A SHELF,
BY MYSELF IN A LONELY ROOM.

*(Rising.)*

BUT WHEN THERE'S A MOON IN MY WINDER
AND IT SLANTS DOWN A BEAM 'CROST MY BED,
THEN THE SHADDER OF A TREE STARTS A-DANCIN' ON
THE WALL
AND A DREAM STARTS A-DANCIN' IN MY HEAD.

AND ALL THE THINGS THAT I WISH FER

TURN OUT LIKE I WANT THEM TO BE,
AND I'M BETTER'N THAT SMART ALECK COWHAND
WHO THINKS HE IS BETTER'N ME
AND THE GIRL THAT I WANT
AIN'T AFRAID OF MY ARMS,
AND HER OWN SOFT ARMS KEEP ME WARM.
AND HER LONG, WAVY* HAIR
FALLS ACROST MY FACE
JIST LIKE THE RAIN IN A STORM!

THE FLOOR CREAKS,
THE DOOR SQUEAKS,
AND THE MOUSE STARTS A-NIBBLIN' ON THE BROOM.
AND THE SUN FLICKS MY EYES –
IT WAS ALL A PACK O' LIES!
I'M AWAKE IN A LONELY ROOM...

I AIN'T GONNA DREAM 'BOUT HER ARMS NO MORE!
I AIN'T GONNA LEAVE HER ALONE!
GOIN' OUTSIDE,
GIT MYSELF A BRIDE,
GIT ME A WOMERN TO CALL MY OWN.

### [MUSIC NO. 16 "CHANGE OF SCENE"]

---

*Original: "yeller."

## Scene Three
## A Grove on Laurey's Farm

*(At Rise: A grove on Laurey's farm. Small groups of YOUNG WOMEN are relaxing, chatting and gossiping. One group watches VIVIAN tell the fortune of a GIRL seated on a stool. To their left, GERTIE observes them.)*

## [MUSIC NO. 17A "DREAM SEQUENCE: MELOS"]

VIVIAN. *(Taking a card from the deck.)* ...And in your future I see a dark, handsome man.

*(Laughter from GIRLS. LAUREY enters.)*

LAUREY. Girls, could you – could you go som'eres else and tell fortunes? I gotta be here by myself.

GERTIE. *(Pointing to bottle.)* Look! She bought 'at ole smellin' salts the peddler tried to sell us!

LAUREY. It ain't smellin' salts. It's goin' to make up my mind fer me. Lookit me take a good whiff now!

*(She coughs.)*

GERTIE. That's the camphor.

*(She exits laughing.)*

LAUREY. Please, girls, go away.

*(The GIRL on the stool rises as the group reforms. LAUREY closes her eyes tight.)*

ELLEN. Hey, Laurey, is it true you're lettin' Jud take you tonight 'stid of Curly?

*(This captures the attention of the other GIRLS.)*

LAUREY. *(Moves to stool as she speaks.)* Tell you better when I think ever'thin' out clear.

*(She sits.)*

Beginnin' to see things clear a'ready.

*(Two of the* **GIRLS** *rise in place. As the singing continues the* **WOMEN** *move closer to* **LAUREY.***)*

**KATE.** I c'n tell you whut you want...

## [MUSIC NO. 17B "DREAM SEQUENCE OUT OF MY DREAMS"]

OUT OF YOUR DREAMS
AND INTO HIS ARMS
YOU LONG TO FLY.

**ELLEN.**

YOU DON'T NEED
EGYPTIAN SMELLIN' SALTS
TO TELL YOU WHY!

**KATE.**

OUT OF YOUR DREAMS
AND INTO THE HUSH
OF FALLING SHADOWS.

**VIRGINIA.**

WHEN THE MIST IS LOW,
AND STARS ARE BREAKING THROUGH,

**VIVIAN.**

THEN OUT OF YOUR DREAMS YOU'LL GO –

**ALL FOUR GIRLS.**

INTO A DREAM COME TRUE.

**ALL GIRLS.** *(Moving quickly, they surround* **LAUREY,** *those closest to her, kneeling.)*

MAKE UP YOUR MIND,
MAKE UP YOUR MIND, LAUREY,
LAUREY DEAR.
MAKE UP YOUR OWN,
MAKE UP YOUR OWN STORY,
LAUREY DEAR.

OLE PHARAOH'S
DAUGHTER WON'T TELL YOU
WHAT TO DO.
ASK YOUR HEART –
WHATEVER IT TELLS YOU WILL BE TRUE.

*(They drift off as* **LAUREY** *sings.)*

**LAUREY.**

> OUT OF MY DREAMS
> AND INTO YOUR ARMS
> I LONG TO FLY.
> I WILL COME AS EVENING COMES
> TO WOO A WAITING SKY.
>
> OUT OF MY DREAMS
> AND INTO THE HUSH
> OF FALLING SHADOWS –

> > (**CURLY** *enters in another spot, walking slowly and standing perfectly still. In the original production,* **LAUREY**, **CURLY**, *and* **JUD** *had ballet counterparts that entered at this point and took over the dancing. Some modern productions have used the same actors who play the roles to perform the ballet. Either way is fine.*)

WHEN THE MIST IS LOW,
AND STARS ARE BREAKING THROUGH,

> > (*The dancing counterparts of* **LAUREY** *and* **CURLY** *enter and stand behind their originals, duplicating their gestures.*)

THEN OUT OF MY DREAMS I'LL GO,
INTO A DREAM WITH YOU.

> > (*The real* **CURLY** *and the real* **LAUREY** *back off slowly and leave the stage to their counterparts, who move toward each other and meet center. The scenery flies, leaving an empty stage.*)

### [MUSIC NO. 17C "DREAM SEQUENCE: INTERLUDE TO BALLET"]

### [MUSIC NO. 17D "DREAM SEQUENCE: BALLET"]

> (*The things* **LAUREY** *sees in her dream that help her make up her mind.*)

(*These dream figures of* **LAUREY** *and* **CURLY** *dance ecstatically. A* **YOUNG GIRL** *enters, sees them, and bounds off to break the news, and soon others dance on and off gaily. Two of* **CURLY'S COWBOY FRIENDS** *stroll by and wave their greeting.* **CURLY** *kisses* **LAUREY** *again and walks away, happy and smug.*)

(*A* **LITTLE GIRL** *runs on, presents* **LAUREY** *with a nosegay, and then bursts into tears. More* **GIRL FRIENDS** *dance in and embrace her. A bridal veil floats down from the skies, and they place it on her head.* **CURLY** *and the* **BOYS** *enter, in the manner of cowboys astride their horses. Following a gay dance, the music slows to wedding-march tempo.* **CURLY,** *a serious expression on his face, awaits his bride, who walks down an aisle formed by the* **GIRLS.**)

(*Now the ballet counterpart of* **JUD** *walks slowly forward and takes off* **LAUREY'S** *veil. Expecting to see her lover,* **CURLY,** *she looks up and finds* **JUD.** *Horrified, she backs away. Her friends, with stony faces, look straight ahead of them.* **CURLY,** *too, is stern and austere, and when* **LAUREY** *appeals to him, he backs away from her. All of them leave her. She is alone with* **JUD.**)

(**JUD** *starts to dance with* **LAUREY,** *but he is soon diverted by the entrance of three* **DANCE-HALL GIRLS** *who look very much like the* Police Gazette *pictures* **LAUREY** *has seen tacked on to Jud's walls in the smokehouse. Some of the* **COWBOYS** *follow the* **GIRLS** *on, and whistle at them. But that is as far as they go. The* **COWBOYS** *are timid and inexpert in handling these sophisticated* **WOMEN.** *The* **WOMEN** *do an amusing, satirically bawdy dance. Then* **JUD** *and the* **BOYS** *dance with them.*)

*(After the* **GIRLS** *dance off,* **LAUREY** *and* **JUD** *are again alone.* **CURLY** *enters, and the long-awaited conflict with* **JUD** *is now unavoidable.* **CURLY,** *his hand holding an imaginary pistol, fires at* **JUD** *again and again, but* **JUD** *keeps slowly advancing on him, immune to the bullets. A fierce fight ensues. The* **FRIENDS** *of* **LAUREY** *and* **CURLY** *run helplessly from one side to the other. Just when the tables seem to have turned in* **CURLY**'s *favor,* **JUD** *gets a death grip on his throat. He is killing* **CURLY.** **LAUREY** *runs up to him and begs him to release her lover. It is clear by her pantomime that she will give herself to* **JUD** *to save* **CURLY.** **JUD** *drops* **CURLY**'s *limp body, picks up* **LAUREY,** *and carries her away. Over* **JUD**'s *shoulder she blows a feeble, heartbroken kiss to* **CURLY**'s *prostrate form on the ground. The* **CROWD** *surrounds him, masking his body, and exiting with him in the dark as a spot comes up, revealing the real* **LAUREY** *being shaken out of her dream by the real* **JUD**.)*

**JUD.** Wake up, Laurey. It's time to start fer the party.

*(As* **LAUREY** *awakens and starts mechanically to go with* **JUD,** *the real* **CURLY** *enters expectantly.* **LAUREY** *hesitates.* **JUD** *holds out his arm and scowls. Remembering the disaster of her recent dream, she avoids its reality by taking* **JUD**'s *arm and going with him, looking wistfully back at* **CURLY** *with the same sad eyes that her ballet counterpart had on her exit.* **CURLY** *stands alone, puzzled, dejected, and defeated, as the curtain falls.)*

# ACT II

[MUSIC NO. 18 "ENTR'ACTE"]

[MUSIC NO. 19 "THE FARMER AND THE COWMAN"]

### Scene One
### The Skidmore Ranch

*(The Skidmore ranch. Skidmore's* **GUESTS** *are dancing a "set" as the curtain rises.)*

*(In the original production, the* **DANCERS** *started dancing eight bars before the curtain came up so that they would be in full swing at curtain. The audience could hear them talking and laughing before the curtain rose.)*

*(The melody settles into a "vamp," and* **CARNES** *holds up his hand as a signal that he wants to sing. The* **DANCERS** *scatter and* **CARNES** *takes over.)*

**CARNES.**

THE FARMER AND THE COWMAN SHOULD BE FRIENDS,
OH, THE FARMER AND THE COWMAN SHOULD BE
    FRIENDS.
ONE MAN LIKES TO PUSH A PLOUGH,
THE OTHER LIKES TO CHASE A COW,
BUT THAT'S NO REASON WHY THEY CAIN'T BE FRIENDS.

TERRITORY FOLKS SHOULD STICK TOGETHER,
TERRITORY FOLKS SHOULD ALL BE PALS.
COWBOYS, DANCE WITH THE FARMERS' DAUGHTERS!
FARMERS, DANCE WITH THE RANCHERS' GALS!

**CHORUS.** *(Dancing as they sing.)*
> TERRITORY FOLKS SHOULD STICK TOGETHER,
> TERRITORY FOLKS SHOULD ALL BE PALS.
> COWBOYS, DANCE WITH THE FARMERS' DAUGHTERS!
> FARMERS, DANCE WITH THE RANCHERS' GALS!

**CARNES.**
> I'D LIKE TO SAY A WORD FER THE FARMER.

**AUNT ELLER.** Well, say it!

**CARNES.**
> HE COME OUT WEST AND MADE A LOT OF CHANGES.

**WILL.** *(Scornfully; singing.)*
> HE COME OUT WEST AND BUILT A LOT OF FENCES!

**CURLY.**
> AND BUILT 'EM RIGHT ACROST OUR CATTLE RANGES!

**CORD ELAM.** *(A cowman.)* Whyn't those dirtscratchers stay in Missouri where they belong?

**FARMER.** We got as much right here –

**CARNES.** *(Shouting.)* Gentlemen – shut up!

> *(Quiet restored, he resumes singing.)*

> THE FARMER IS A GOOD AND THRIFTY CITIZEN.

**FRED.** He's thrifty, all right.

**CARNES.** *(Glaring at* **FRED,** *he continues with song.)*
> NO MATTER WHUT THE COWMAN SAYS OR THINKS,
> YOU SELDOM SEE 'IM DRINKIN' IN A BAR ROOM –

**CURLY.**
> UNLESS SOMEBODY ELSE IS BUYIN' DRINKS!

**CARNES.** *(Barging in quickly to save the party's respectability.)*
> BUT THE FARMER AND THE COWMAN SHOULD BE
>     FRIENDS,
> OH, THE FARMER AND THE COWMAN SHOULD BE
>     FRIENDS.
> THE COWMAN ROPES A COW WITH EASE,
> THE FARMER STEALS HER BUTTER AND CHEESE,
> BUT THAT'S NO REASON WHY THEY CAIN'T BE FRIENDS!

**ALL.**
> TERRITORY FOLKS SHOULD STICK TOGETHER,

TERRITORY FOLKS SHOULD ALL BE PALS.
COWBOYS, DANCE WITH THE FARMERS' DAUGHTERS!
FARMERS, DANCE WITH THE RANCHERS' GALS!

*(On the vamp, the* **DANCERS** *bow to* **CARNES** *and skip back to place.)*

**AUNT ELLER.**

I'D LIKE TO SAY A WORD FER THE COWBOY...

**FARMER.** *(Anxious to get back at the cowmen.)* Oh, you would!

**AUNT ELLER.**

THE ROAD HE TREADS IS DIFFICULT AND STONY.
HE RIDES FER DAYS ON END
WITH JIST A PONY FER A FRIEND...

**ADO ANNIE.**

I SHORE AM FEELIN' SORRY FER THE PONY!

**AUNT ELLER.**

THE FARMER SHOULD BE SOCIABLE WITH THE COWBOY,
IF HE RIDES BY AND ASKS FER FOOD AND WATER.

*(Parlando.)*

DON'T TREAT HIM LIKE A LOUSE,
MAKE HIM WELCOME IN YER HOUSE...

**CARNES.**

BUT BE SHORE THAT YOU LOCK UP YER WIFE AN' DAUGHTER!

*(Laughs, jibes, protests.)*

**CORD ELAM.** Who wants a ole farm womern anyway?

**ADO ANNIE.** Notice you married one, so's you c'd git a square meal!

**MAN.** *(To* **CORD ELAM.***)* You cain't talk that-a-way 'bout our womern folks!

**WILL.** He can say whut he wants.

*(He hauls off on* **CORD**, *and a free-for-all fight ensues, all the* **MEN** *mixing with one another, the* **WOMEN** *striving vainly to keep peace by singing.)*

**ALL (WHO ARE NOT FIGHTING).**

OH, THE FARMER AND THE COWMAN SHOULD BE
FRIENDS,
THE FARMER AND THE COWMAN SHOULD BE...(FRIENDS.)

(**AUNT ELLER**, *who has grabbed* **CORD***'s gun
during the fight, fires it. This freezes the
picture. A still, startled* **CROWD** *stops and
looks to see who's been shot.* **AUNT ELLER**
*strides forward, separating the* **FIGHTERS**,
*pulling them away from one another, and
none too gently.*)

**AUNT ELLER.** They ain't nobody goin' to slug out anythin' –
this here's a party!

(*Pointing the gun at* **CARNES**.*)

Sing it, Andrew!
DUM TIDDY UM TUM TUM –

**CARNES.** (*Frightened, he obeys.*)

THE FARMER AND THE COWMAN SHOULD BE FRIENDS...

(**AUNT ELLER** *points her gun at a* **GROUP** *and
conducts them. They join in quickly.*)

**RIGHT GROUP.**

OH, THE FARMER AND THE COWMAN SHOULD BE
FRIENDS.

(**AUNT ELLER** *turns her gun on the* **LEFT GROUP**,
*and now they all sing.*)

**ALL.**

ONE MAN LIKES TO PUSH A PLOUGH,
THE OTHER LIKES TO CHASE A COW,
BUT THAT'S NO REASON WHY THEY CAIN'T BE FRIENDS!

(**CURLY** *comes down and joins* **AUNT ELLER**
*and* **CARNES**.*)

**IKE.**

AND WHEN THIS TERRITORY IS A STATE,
AN' JINES THE UNION JIST LIKE ALL THE OTHERS,
THE FARMER AND THE COWMAN AND THE MERCHANT
MUST ALL BEHAVE THEIRSEL'S AND ACT LIKE BROTHERS.

*(The music becomes slower and quieter.)*

**AUNT ELLER.**

I'D LIKE TO TEACH YOU ALL A LITTLE SAYIN' –
AND LEARN THESE WORDS BY HEART THE WAY YOU
   SHOULD:
"I DON'T SAY I'M NO BETTER THAN ANYBODY ELSE,

   *(Music up again. The tempo here should set
   the tempo of the dance which follows.)*

BUT I'LL BE DAMNED IF I AIN'T JIST AS GOOD!"

   *(They cheer the sentiment and repeat lustily.)*

**ALL.**

I DON'T SAY I'M NO BETTER THAN ANYBODY ELSE,
BUT I'LL BE DAMNED IF I AIN'T JIST AS GOOD!

TERRITORY FOLKS SHOULD STICK TOGETHER,
TERRITORY FOLKS SHOULD ALL BE PALS.
COWBOYS, DANCE WITH THE FARMERS' DAUGHTERS!
FARMERS, DANCE WITH THE RANCHERS' GALS!

   *(Now they go into a gay, unrestrained dance.)*

**[MUSIC NO. 20 "FARMER DANCE"]**

TERRITORY FOLKS SHOULD STICK TOGETHER,
TERRITORY FOLKS SHOULD ALL BE PALS.
COWBOYS, DANCE WITH THE FARMERS' DAUGHTERS!

   *(Singing, with a big ritard at the end.)*

FARMERS, DANCE WITH THE RANCHERS' GALS!

**IKE.** *(After number is over.)* C'mon, everybody! Time to start the Box Social.

**CORD ELAM.** I'm so hungry I c'd eat a gatepost.

**GIRL.** Who's goin' to be the auctioneer?

**MAN.** Aunt Eller!

   *(Shouts of approval from the entire crowd.)*

**AUNT ELLER.** *(Playing coy.)* Let one of the men be the auctioneer.

**CROWD.** *(Ad-libs.)* "No, Aunt Eller, yore the best." "Ain't any ole men auctioneers as good as you."

**AUNT ELLER.** All right then. Now you know the rules, gentlemen. Y'got to bid blind. Y'ain't s'posed to know whut girl goes with whut hamper. Of course, if yer sweetheart has told you that hers'll be done up in a certain kind of way with a certain color ribbon, that ain't my fault. Now we'll auction all the hampers on t'other side of the house and work around back here. Follow me.

> (*She starts off, followed by the* **CROWD**. *As the* **CROWD** *exits,* **ALI HAKIM** *strolls on, meeting* **WILL** *ambling along with his bag.*)

**ALI HAKIM.** Hello, young fellow.

**WILL.** Oh, it's you!

**ALI HAKIM.** I was just hoping to meet up with you. It seems like you and me ought to have a little talk.

**WILL.** We only got one thing to talk about. Well, Mr. Hakim, I hear you got yourself engaged to Ado Annie.

**ALI HAKIM.** Well...

**WILL.** Well, nuthin'. I don't know what to call you. You ain't purty enough fer a skunk. You ain't skinny enough fer a snake. You're too little to be a man, and too big to be a mouse. I reckon you're a rat.

**ALI HAKIM.** That's logical.

**WILL.** Answer me one question. Do you really love her?

**ALI HAKIM.** Well...

**WILL.** Cuz if I thought you didn't I'd tie you up in this bag and drop you in the river. Are you serious about her?

**ALI HAKIM.** Yes, I'm serious.

**WILL.** And do you worship the ground she walks on, like I do?

> (*He grabs* **ALI** *at his throat, almost lifting him off the ground.*)

And this is one answer that better be yes.

**ALI HAKIM.** Yes – yes – yes.

**WILL.** (*Releasing* **ALI**.) The hell you do!

**ALI HAKIM.** Yes.

**WILL.** Would you spend every cent you had fer her? That's whut I did. See that bag? Full of presents. Cost fifty bucks. All I had in the world.

**ALI HAKIM.** If you had that fifty dollars cash...

**WILL.** I'd have Ado Annie, and you'd lose her.

**ALI HAKIM.** *(Thoughtfully.)* Yes. I'd lose her. Let's see what you got in here. Might want to buy something.

**WILL.** What would you want with them?

**ALI HAKIM.** I'm a peddler, ain't I? I buy and sell. Maybe pay you real money...

*(Significantly.)* Maybe as much as – well, a lot.

> (**WILL** *becomes thoughtful.* **ALI** *fishes in the bag and pulls out an item.*)

Ah, what a beautiful hot-water bag. Looks French. Must have cost plenty. I'll give you eight dollars for it.

**WILL.** Eight dollars? That wouldn't be honest. I only paid three-fifty.

**ALI HAKIM.** All right. I said I'd give you eight and I will...

> (*He pulls a nightgown out of the bag. It is made of white lace and is notable for a profusion of ribbons and bows on the neckline.*)

Say! That's a cracker-jake!

**WILL.** Take your hands off that!

> (*Grabbing it and holding it in front of him.*)

That wuz fer our weddin' night!

**ALI HAKIM.** It don't fit you so good. I'll pay you twenty-two dollars.

**WILL.** But that's –

**ALI HAKIM.** All right then – twenty-two-fifty!

> (*Stuffing it into his coat with the hot-water bag.*)

Not a cent more.

*(WILL smiles craftily and starts to count on his fingers. ALI now pulls out a corset.)*

**WILL.** Them – those – that was fer her to wear.

**ALI HAKIM.** I didn't hardly think they was for you.

*(Looking at it.)*

Mighty dainty.

*(Putting it aside.)*

Fifteen dollars. Le's see, eight and twenty-two makes thirty and fifteen is forty-five and fifty cents is forty-five-fifty.

*(He looks craftily at WILL out of the corner of his eye and watches the idea percolate through WILL's thick head.)*

**WILL.** Forty-five-fifty? Say, that's almos' – that's...

*(Turning anxiously.)*

Want to buy some more?

**ALI HAKIM.** Might.

**WILL.** *(Taking "The Little Wonder" out of his pocket.)* D'you ever see one of these?

**ALI HAKIM.** *(Frightened.)* What made you buy this? Got it *in* for somebody?

**WILL.** How d'you mean? It's jist funny pitchers.

**ALI HAKIM.** *(Examining it carefully.)* That all you think it is? Well, it's more'n that! It's...

*(He breaks off as LAUREY runs on, a frightened look on her face.)*

**LAUREY.** Whur is ev'ybody? Whur's Aunt Eller?

**WILL.** On t'other side of the house, Laurey.

**JUD.** *(Offstage.)* Laurey! Whur'd you run to?

*(LAUREY runs off around the end of the house, putting her hamper on the porch.)*

**WILL.** How much'll you give me fer this thing?

**ALI HAKIM**. I don't like to handle things like this. I guess you don't know what it really is.

**WILL**. Shore do. It's jist a girl in pink tights.

(**JUD** *enters.*)

**JUD**. Either of you two see Laurey?

**WILL**. Just went to th' other side of the house. Auction's goin' on there.

(**JUD** *grunts and starts upstage.*)

**ALI HAKIM**. (*Calling to him.*) Hey, Jud! Here's one of them things you was looking for. "The Little Wonder."

(**JUD** *comes back and examines it.*)

**JUD**. (*To* **WILL**.) How much?

**WILL**. (*Closing his eyes to struggle with a mathematical problem.*) Three dollars and fifty cents.

**JUD**. (*Digging in his pocket.*) Lotta money but I got an idy it might be worth it.

(*He goes upstage to look it over, then exits.*)

**WILL**. Let's see, three-fifty from him and forty-five-fifty from you. 'At makes fifty dollars, don't it?

**ALI HAKIM**. No. One dollar short.

(*He gives the bag a sly kick, so that it lands in front of* **WILL**.)

**WILL**. Darn it. I musta figgered wrong.
(*Impulsively.*) How much fer all the resta the stuff in this bag?

**ALI HAKIM**. (*Having the cash all ready, he hands* **WILL** *the dollar bill.*) One dollar!

**WILL**. Done! Now I got fifty dollars, ain't I? Know whut that means? Means I'm goin' to take Ado Annie back from you!

**ALI HAKIM**. You wouldn't do a thing like that to me!

**WILL**. Oh, wouldn't I? And when I tell her paw who I got mosta the money offa, mebbe he'll change his mind 'bout who's smart and who's dumb!

**ALI HAKIM.** Say, young feller, you certainly bunkoed me!

> *(There is a hum of voices heard from offstage, and the* **CROWD** *briskly returns for the final bidding.* **AUNT ELLER** *enters, followed by the balance of the party. One of the men sets Laurey and Ado Annie's hampers in front of where* **AUNT ELLER** *will be conducting the auction.* **CURLY** *stands apart and pays little attention to anybody or anything.)*

**AUNT ELLER.** Now, here's the last two hampers. Whose they are I ain't got no idy!

**ADO ANNIE.** *(In a loud voice.)* The littel un's mine! And the one next to it is Laurey's!

> *(General laughter.)*

**AUNT ELLER.** Well, that's the end of *that* secret. Now whut am I bid fer Ado Annie's hamper?

**SLIM.** Two bits.

**CORD ELAM.** Four.

**AUNT ELLER.** Who says six? You, Slim?

> *(***SLIM*** shakes his head.)*

Ain't nobody hungry no more? – Whut about you, Peddler-man? Six bits?

> *(Pause.)*

**ALI HAKIM.** Naw!

> *(***CARNES*** takes a gun from his pocket and prods* **ALI** *in the back.)*

**CARNES.** Come on.

**ALI HAKIM.** Six bits!

**AUNT ELLER.** Six bits ain't enough fer a lunch like Ado Annie c'n make. Le's hear a dollar. How about you, Mike? You won her last year.

**MIKE.** Yeah. That's right. Hey, Ado Annie, y' got that same sweet-pertater pie like last year?

**ADO ANNIE.** You bet.

**AUNT ELLER.** Same old sweet-pertater pie, Mike. Whut d'you say?

**MIKE.** I say it give me a three-day bellyache!

**AUNT ELLER.** Never mind about that. Who bids a dollar?

**CARNES.** *(Whispering to* **ALI HAKIM.**) Bid!

**ALI HAKIM.** *(Whispering it back.)* Mine's the last bid. I got her fer six bits.

**CARNES.** Bid a dollar.

> *(***ALI*** looks doubtful.* **CARNES** *prods him with his gun.)*

**ALI HAKIM.** Ninety cents.

**AUNT ELLER.** Ninety cents, we're gittin' rich. 'Nother desk fer th' schoolhouse. Do I hear more?

**WILL.** *(Dramatically.)* You hear fifty dollars!

**ALI HAKIM.** *(Immediately alarmed.)* Hey!

**AUNT ELLER.** Fifty dollars! Nobody ever bid fifty dollars for a lunch! Nobody ever bid ten.

**CARNES.** He ain't got fifty dollars.

**WILL.** Oh, yes, I have.

> *(Producing the money.)*

And 'f yer a man of honor y'gotta say Ado Annie b'longs to me, like y'said she would!

**CARNES.** But where's yer money?

**WILL.** *(Shoving out his hand.)* Right here in my hand.

**CARNES.** 'At ain't yours! Y'jist bid it, didn't you? Just give it to th' schoolhouse.

> *(To* **ALI,** *chuckling back to* **WILL.**) Got to say the peddler still gits my daughter's hand.

**WILL.** Now wait a minute. That ain't fair!

**AUNT ELLER.** Goin' fer fifty dollars! Goin'...

**ALI HAKIM.** *(Gulping.)* Fifty-one!

> *(A sensation, all turn to* **ALI.**)

**CARNES.** You crazy?

**WILL.** *(Mechanically.)* Fif–

*(Prompted by frantic signs from* **ALI**, *he stops and suddenly realizes the significance of* **ALI***'s bid.)*

**WILL.** Wait a minute. Wait! 'F I don't bid any more I c'n keep my money, cain't I?

**AUNT ELLER.** *(Grinning.)* Shore can.

**WILL.** Nen I still got fifty dollars.

*(Waving it in front of* **CARNES**.*)*

This is mine!

**CARNES.** *(To* **ALI HAKIM**.*)* You feeble-minded shike-poke!

**AUNT ELLER.** Goin', goin', gone fer fifty-one dollars and 'at means Ado Annie'll git the prize, I guess.

**WILL.** And I git Ado Annie!

**CARNES.** *(To* **ALI HAKIM**.*)* And whut're you gittin' fer yer fifty-one dollars?

**ALI HAKIM.** *(***ADO ANNIE** *hands him her hamper. He speaks dead front.)* A three-day bellyache!

*(***ALI** *and* **ADO ANNIE** *leave.* **JUD** *enters up right and stands in back of crowd.)*

**AUNT ELLER.** Now here's my niece's hamper.

*(General murmur of excitement runs through the* **CROWD**.*)*

I took a peek inside a while ago and I must say it looks mighty tasty. Whut do I hear, gents?

**SLIM.** Two bits!

**FRED.** Four bits!

**AUNT ELLER.** Whut d'you say, Slim? Six?

*(***SLIM** *shakes his head.)*

**CARNES.** I bid one dollar.

**AUNT ELLER.** More like it! Do I hear two?

**JUD.** A dollar and a quarter.

*(***LAUREY** *is startled by his voice.)*

**CORD ELAM.** Two dollars.

**JOE.** Two-fifty.

**CARNES.** Three dollars!

**JUD.** And two bits.

**CORD ELAM.** Three dollars and four bits!

**JOE.** Four dollars.

**JUD.** *(Doggedly.)* And two bits.

> *(**LAUREY** looks straight ahead, grimly. **AUNT ELLER** catches this look and a deep worry comes into her eyes.)*

**AUNT ELLER.** Four and a quarter.

> *(Looking at **CURLY**, an appeal in her voice.)*

Ain't I goin' to hear any more?

> *(**CURLY** turns and walks off, cool, deliberate. **LAUREY** bites her lip. **AUNT ELLER**'s voice has panic in it.)*

I got a bid of four and a quarter – from Jud Fry. You goin' to let him have it?

**CARNES.** Four and a half.

**AUNT ELLER.** *(Shouting, as if she were cheering.)* Four and a half! Goin' fer four and a half! Goin'...

**JUD.** Four seventy-five.

**AUNT ELLER.** *(Deflated.)* Four seventy-five. Come on, gentlemen. Schoolhouse ain't built yet. Got to git a nice chimbley.

**CORD ELAM.** Five dollars.

**AUNT ELLER.** Goin' fer five dollars! Goin'...

**JUD.** And two bits.

**CORD ELAM.** Too rich for my blood! Cain't afford no more.

**AUNT ELLER.** *(Worried.)* Five and a quarter! Ain't got nearly enough yet.

> *(Looking at **CARNES**.)*

Not fer cold duck with stuffin' and that lemon-meringue pie.

**CARNES.** Six dollars.

**AUNT ELLER.** Six dollars! Goin'...

**JUD.** And two bits.

**AUNT ELLER.** My, you're stubborn, Jud. Mr. Carnes is a richer man'n you.

> *(Looking at* **CARNES.***)*

And I know he likes custard with raspberry syrup.

> *(Pause. No one bids.)*

Anybody goin' to bid any more?

**JUD.** No. They all dropped out. Cain't you see?

**FRED.** You got enough, Aunt Eller.

**CARNES.** Let's git on.

**JUD.** Here's the money.

**AUNT ELLER.** *(Looking off.)* Hold on, you! I ain't said, "Goin', goin', gone" yet!

**JUD.** Well, say it!

**AUNT ELLER.** *(Speaking slowly.)* Goin' to Jud Fry fer six dollars and two bits! Goin'...

> *(***CURLY** *enters, a saddle over his arm.)*

**CURLY.** Who'd you say was gittin' Laurey?

**AUNT ELLER.** Jud Fry.

**CURLY.** And fer how much?

**AUNT ELLER.** Six and a quarter.

**CURLY.** I don't figger 'at's quite enough, do you?

**JUD.** It's more'n *you* got.

**CURLY.** Got a saddle here cost me thirty dollars.

**JUD.** Yo' cain't bid saddles. Got to be cash.

**CURLY.** *(Looking around.)* Thirty-dollar saddle must be worth sumpin to somebody.

**JOE.** I'll give you ten.

**SKIDMORE.** *(To* **CURLY.***)* Don't be a fool, boy. Y'cain't earn a livin' 'thout a saddle.

**CURLY.** *(To* **JOE.***)* Got cash?

**JOE.** Right in my pocket.

*(**CURLY** gives him the saddle.)*

**CURLY.** *(Turning to **JUD**.)* Don't let's waste time. How high you goin'?

**JUD.** Higher'n you – no matter whut!

**CURLY.** *(To **AUNT ELLER**.)* Aunt Eller, I'm biddin' all of this ten dollars Joe jist give me.

**AUNT ELLER.** Ten dollars – goin'...

> *(Pause. General murmur of excited comments. **LAUREY**'s eyes are shining now and her shoulders are straighter.)*

**JUD.** *(Determinedly.)* Ten dollars *and* two bits.

**AUNT ELLER.** Curly...

> *(Pause. **CURLY** turns to a group of **MEN**.)*

**CURLY.** Most of you boys know my horse, Dun. She's a –

> *(He swallows hard.)*

– a kinda nice horse – gentle and well broke.

**LAUREY.** Don't sell Dun, Curly, it ain't worth it.

**CORD ELAM.** I'll give you twenty-five fer her!

**CURLY.** *(To **CORD ELAM**.)* I'll sell Dun to you.

*(To **AUNT ELLER**.)* That makes the bid thirty-five, Aunt Eller.

**AUNT ELLER.** *(Tickled to death.)* Curly, yer crazy! But it's all fer the schoolhouse, ain't it? All fer educatin' and larnin'. Goin' fer thirty-five. Goin' –

**JUD.** Hold on! I ain't finished biddin'!

> *(He grins fiercely at **CURLY**.)*

You jist put up everythin' y'got in the world, didn't yer? Cain't bid your clothes, cuz they ain't worth nuthin'. Cain't bid yer gun cuz you need that.

> *(Slowly.)*

Yes, sir. You need that bad.

> *(Looking at **AUNT ELLER**.)*

**JUD.** So, Aunt Eller, I'm jist as reckless as Curly McLain, I guess. Just as good at gittin' whut I want. Goin' to bid all I got in the world – all I saved fer two years, doin' farm work. All fer Laurey. Here it is! Forty-two dollars and thirty-one cents.

*(He pours the money out of a pouch he has taken from his pocket onto Laurey's hamper.* **CURLY** *takes out his gun. The crowd gasps.* **JUD** *backs away.)*

**CURLY.** Anybody want to buy a gun? You, Joe? Bought it brand new last Thanksgivin'. Worth a lot.

**LAUREY.** Curly, please don't sell your gun.

*(***CURLY*** *looks at* ***SLIM.****)*

**SLIM.** Give you eighteen dollars fer it.

**CURLY.** Sold.

*(They settle the deal.* **CURLY** *turns to* **AUNT ELLER.***)*

That makes my bid fifty-three dollars, Aunt Eller.
*(Significantly.)* Anybody going any higher?

**AUNT ELLER.** *(Very quickly.)* Goin' – goin' – gone! Whut's the matter with you folks? Ain't nobody gonna cheer er nuthin'?

*(Uncertainly, they start to sing "The Farmer and the Cowman" a cappella.* **JUD** *picks up his money.* **CURLY** *and* **LAUREY** *carry their basket downstage and away from the crowd.* **JUD** *moves slowly toward* **CURLY.** **CURLY** *sets the basket down and faces him. The singing stops.)*

**SKIDMORE.** *(In his deep, booming voice.)* That's the idy! The cowman and the farmer shud be friends.

*(His hand on* **JUD**'s *shoulder.)*

You lost the bid, but the biddin' was fair.
*(To* **CURLY.***)* C'mon, cowman – shake the farmer's hand!

(**CURLY** *doesn't move a muscle.*)

**JUD**. Shore, I'll shake hands. No hard feelin's, Curly.

> (*He goes to* **CURLY**, *his hand outstretched. After a pause,* **CURLY** *takes his hand, but never lets his eyes leave* **JUD***'s.*)

**SKIDMORE**. That's better.

> (**ALI** *has come downstage and is watching* **JUD** *narrowly.*)

**JUD**. (*With a badly assumed manner of camaraderie.*) Say, Curly, I want to show you sumpin.

> (*He grins.*)

'Scuseus, Laurey.

> (*Taking* **CURLY***'s arm, he leads him aside.*)

Ever see one of these things?

> (*He takes out "The Little Wonder."* **ALI** *is in a panic.*)

**CURLY**. Just whut *is* that?

> (**ALI** *rushes to* **AUNT ELLER** *and starts to whisper in her ear.*)

**JUD**. Something special. You jist put this up to yer eye like this, see?

> (**CURLY** *is about to look when* **AUNT ELLER***'s voice rings out, sharp and shrill.*)

**AUNT ELLER**. Curly! Curly, whut you doin'?

> (**CURLY** *turns quickly. So does* **JUD**, *giving an involuntary grunt of disappointment.*)

**CURLY**. Doin'? Nuthin' much. Whut you want to squeal at a man like 'at fer? Skeer the liver and lights out of a feller.

**AUNT ELLER**. Well then, stop lookin' at those ole French pitchers and ast me fer a dance. You brung me to the party, didn't you?

**CURLY**. All right then, you silly ole woman, I'll dance 'th you. Dance you all over the meadow, you want!

**AUNT ELLER**. Pick 'at banjo to pieces, Sam!

### [MUSIC NO. 21 "CHANGE OF SCENE"]

*(And the dance is on. Everyone is dancing now.* **WILL** *takes* **ADO ANNIE** *by the waist and swings her around.* **JUD**, *finally realizing the chance to use "The Little Wonder" is gone, angrily slips it back into his pocket, then goes up to* **LAUREY**, *who has started to dance with* **ALI**. **JUD** *pushes* **ALI** *away and dances* **LAUREY** *off.* **ALI** *and the remaining* **COMPANY** *drift off, leaving* **WILL** *and* **ADO ANNIE** *alone.* **WILL** *wants to settle things.)*

**WILL**. Well, Ado Annie, I got the fifty dollars cash, now you name the day.

**ADO ANNIE**. August fifteenth.

**WILL**. Why August fifteenth?

**ADO ANNIE**. *(Reminiscing.)* That was the first day I was kissed.

**WILL**. *(His face lighting up.)* Was it? I didn't remember that.

**ADO ANNIE**. You wasn't there.

**WILL**. Now looka here, we gotta have a serious talk. Now that you're engaged to me, you gotta stop havin' fun! ...I mean with other fellers.

### [MUSIC NO. 22 "ALL ER NUTHIN'"]

*(Half-sung.)*

YOU'LL HAVE TO BE A LITTLE MORE STAND-OFFISH

*(Sings.)*

WHEN FELLERS OFFER YOU A BUGGY RIDE.

**ADO ANNIE**.

I'LL GIVE A IMITATION OF A CRAWFISH
AND DIG MYSELF A HOLE WHERE I C'N HIDE.

**WILL.**

I HEARED HOW YOU WAS KICKIN' UP SOME CAPERS
WHEN I WAS OFF IN KANSAS CITY, MO.

*(More sternly.)*

I HEARED SOME THINGS YOU COULDN'T PRINT IN PAPERS
FROM FELLERS WHO BEEN TALKIN' LIKE THEY KNOW!

**ADO ANNIE.**

*(Spoken.)* FOOT!

I ONLY DID THE KIND OF THINGS I ORTA – SORTA
TO YOU I WAS AS FAITHFUL AS C'N BE – FER ME.
THEM STORIES 'BOUT THE WAY I LOST MY BLOOMERS –
RUMORS!
A LOT O' TEMPEST IN A POT O' TEA!

**WILL.**

THE WHOLE THING DON'T SOUND VERY GOOD TO ME –

**ADO ANNIE.** *(Spoken.)*

WELL, Y'SEE –

**WILL.** *(Breaking in and spurting out his pent-up resentment
at a great injustice.)*

*(Parlando.)*

I GO AND SOW MY LAST WILD OAT!
I CUT OUT ALL SHENANIGANS!
I SAVE MY MONEY – DON'T GAMBLE ER DRINK
IN THE BACK ROOM DOWN AT FLANNIGAN'S!

I GIVE UP LOTSA OTHER THINGS
A GENTLEMAN NEVER MENTIONS –
BUT BEFORE I GIVE UP ANY MORE,
I WANTA KNOW YOUR INTENTIONS!

*(Sung.)*

WITH ME IT'S ALL ER NUTHIN'!
IS IT ALL ER NUTHIN' WITH YOU?
IT CAIN'T BE "IN BETWEEN"
IT CAIN'T BE "NOW AND THEN"
NO HALF-AND-HALF ROMANCE WILL DO!

I'M A ONE-WOMAN MAN,
HOME-LOVIN' TYPE,

ALL COMPLETE WITH SLIPPERS AND PIPE.
TAKE ME LIKE I AM ER LEAVE ME BE!

IF YOU CAIN'T GIVE ME ALL, GIVE ME NUTHIN' –
AND NUTHIN'S WHUT YOU'LL GIT FROM ME!

*(He struts away from* **ADO ANNIE**.*)*

**ADO ANNIE.**

NOT EVEN SUMP'N?

**WILL.**

NUTHIN'S WHUT YOU'LL GIT FROM ME!

*(The second refrain begins. He starts to walk away, nonchalantly.* **ADO ANNIE** *follows him.)*

**ADO ANNIE.**

IT CAIN'T BE "IN BETWEEN"?

**WILL.** *(Spoken.)*

UH-UH.

**ADO ANNIE.**

IT CAIN'T BE "NOW AND THEN"?

**WILL.**

NO HALF-AND-HALF ROMANCE WILL DO!

**ADO ANNIE.**

WOULD YOU BUILD ME A HOUSE,
ALL PAINTED WHITE,
CUTE AND CLEAN AND PURTY AND BRIGHT?

**WILL.**

BIG ENOUGH FER TWO BUT NOT FER THREE!

**ADO ANNIE.**

SUPPOSIN' 'AT WE SHOULD HAVE A THIRD ONE?

**WILL.** *(Barking at her.)*

HE BETTER LOOK A LOT LIKE ME!

**ADO ANNIE.** *(Sheered.)*

THE SPIT AN' IMAGE!

**WILL.**

HE BETTER LOOK A LOT LIKE ME!

*(Two* **GIRLS** *come on and do a dance with* **WILL** *in which they lure him away from* **ADO**

**ANNIE. ADO ANNIE,** *trying to get him back, does a Persian dance.* **WILL,** *accusing her, says: "That's Persian!" and returns to the* **GIRLS.** *But* **ADO ANNIE** *yanks him back. The* **GIRLS** *dance off.* **ADO ANNIE** *sings.)*

**ADO ANNIE.**

WITH YOU IT'S ALL ER NUTHIN' –
ALL FER YOU AND NUTHIN' FER ME!
BUT IF A WIFE IS WISE
SHE'S GOTTA REALIZE
THAT MEN LIKE YOU ARE WILD AND FREE.

*(***WILL** *looks pleased.)*

SO I AIN'T GONNA FUSS,
AIN'T GONNA FROWN,
HAVE YOUR FUN, GO OUT ON THE TOWN,
STAY UP LATE AND DON'T COME HOME TILL THREE,
AND GO RIGHT OFF TO SLEEP IF YOU'RE SLEEPY –
THERE'S NO USE WAITIN' UP FER ME!

**WILL.**

OH, ADO ANNIE!

**ADO ANNIE.**

NO USE WAITIN' UP FER ME!

**WILL.**

COME ON AND KISS ME.

*(***ADO ANNIE** *happily returns to* **WILL.** *They kiss and dance off.)*

*(Blackout.)*

**[MUSIC NO. 23 "CHANGE OF SCENE"]**

## Scene Two
## The Kitchen Porch of Skidmore's Ranch House

*(The kitchen porch of Skidmore's ranch house. There are a few benches on the porch and a large coal stove. At Rise: The music for the dance can still be heard offstage. Immediately after the curtain rises,* **JUD** *dances on with* **LAUREY**, *then stops and holds her. She pulls away from him.)*

**LAUREY.** Why we stoppin'? Thought you wanted to dance.

**JUD.** Want to talk to you. What made ya slap that whip onto Old Eighty, and nearly make her run away? Whut was yer hurry?

**LAUREY.** 'Fraid we'd be late fer the party.

**JUD.** You didn't want to be with me by yerself – not a minnit more'n ya had to.

**LAUREY.** Why, I don't know whut you're talking about! I'm with you by myself now, ain't I?

**JUD.** You wouldn'ta been, if ya coulda got out of it. Mornin's you stay hid in yer room all the time. Nights you set in the front room, and won't git outa Aunt Eller's sight... Last time I see ya alone it was winter, with the snow six inches deep in drifts when I was sick. Ya brung me that hot soup out to the smoke house and give it to me, and me in bed. I hadn't shaved in two days. You ast me 'f I had any fever and ya put yer hand on my head to see.

**LAUREY.** *(Puzzled and frightened.)* I remember...

**JUD.** Do ya? Bet ya don't remember as much as me. I remember eve'ything ya ever done...every word ya ever said. Cain't think of nuthin' else... See? ...See how it is.

*(He attempts to hold* **LAUREY**. *She pushes him away.)*

I ain't good enough, am I? I'm a h'ard hand, got dirt on my hands, pigslop. Ain't fitten to tetch ya. You're better, so much better. Yeah, we'll see who's better – Miss Laurey. Nen you'll wisht you wasn't so free with yer airs, yer sich a fine lady...

**LAUREY.** *(Suddenly angry and losing her fear.)* Air you making threats to me? Air you standing there tryin' to tell me 'f I don't 'low you to slobber over me like a hog, why, you're gonna do sumpin 'bout it? Why you're nuthin' but a mangy dog and somebody orta shoot you. You think so much about being a h'ard hand. Well, I'll just tell you sumpin that'll rest your brain, Mr. Jud. You ain't a h'ard hand fer me no more. You c'n just pack up yer duds and scoot. Oh, and I even got better idys'n that. You ain't to come on the place again, you hear me? I'll send yer stuff any place you say, but don't you's much's set foot inside the pasture gate or I'll sic the dogs onto you!

**JUD.** *(Standing quite still, absorbed, dark, his voice low.)* Said yer say! Brought it on yerself. *(In a voice harsh with an inner frenzy.)* Cain't he'p it. Cain't never rest. Told ya the way it was. You wouldn't listen –

> *(He goes out, passes the corner of the house, and disappears.* **LAUREY** *stands a moment, held by his strangeness, then she starts toward the house, changes her mind, and sinks onto a bench, a frightened little girl again. There is a noise offstage.* **LAUREY** *turns, startled.)*

**LAUREY.** Who's 'at?

**WILL.** *(Entering.)* It's me, Laurey. Hey, have you seen Ado Annie? She's *gone agin.*

> *(***LAUREY** *shakes her head.)*

**LAUREY.** *(Calling to him as he is on his way out.)* Will! ... Will, could you do sumpin fer me? Go and find Curly and tell him I'm here.

> *(***CURLY** *enters.)*

I wanta see Curly awful bad. Got to see him.

**CURLY**. Then whyn't you turn around and look, you crazy womern?

**LAUREY**. *(With great relief.)* Curly!

**WILL**. Well, you found yours. I gotta go hunt fer mine.

> *(He exits.)*

**CURLY**. Now whut on earth is ailin' the belle of Claremore? By gum, if you ain't cryin'!

**LAUREY**. *(Leaning against him.)* Curly – I'm afraid, 'fraid of my life!

**CURLY**. *(In a flurry of surprise and delight.)* Jumpin' toadstools!

> *(He puts his arms around **LAUREY**, muttering under his breath.)*

Great Lord!

**LAUREY**. Don't you leave me –

**CURLY**. Great Godamighty!

**LAUREY**. Don't mind me a-cryin', I cain't he'p it...

**CURLY**. Cry yer eyes out!

**LAUREY**. Oh, I don't know whut to do!

**CURLY**. Here. I'll show you.

> *(He lifts **LAUREY**'s face and kisses her gently. The kiss leaves her breathless. She steps back in a state of wonder. Then suddenly she grabs him around the neck and kisses him enthusiastically. He responds, but overcome with a sense of responsibility, he pulls her hands from around his neck and steps back.)*

My goodness!

> *(He shakes his head as if coming out of a daze and gives a low whistle.)*

Whew! 'Bout all a man c'n stand in public!

> *(**LAUREY** lunges for him again.)*

Go 'way from me, *you!*

**LAUREY**. You don't like me, Curly –

**CURLY**. Like you? My God! Git away from me, I tell you, plumb away from me!

> *(He backs away and sits on the stove.)*

**LAUREY**. Curly! You're settin' on the stove!

**CURLY**. *(Leaping up.)* Godamighty!

> *(He turns around, puts his hand down gingerly on the lid.)*

Aw! 'S cold's a hunk of ice!

**LAUREY**. Wish't ud burnt a hole in yer pants.

**CURLY**. *(Grinning at her, understandingly.)* Oh, ya do, do ya?

**LAUREY**. *(Turning away to hide her smile.)* You heared me.

**CURLY**. Laurey, now looky here, you stand over there right whur you air, and I'll set over here – and you tell me whut you wanted with me.

**LAUREY**. *(Grave again.)* Well – Jud was here.

> *(She shudders.)*

He skeered me...he's crazy. I never saw nobody like him. He talked wild and he threatened me. So I – I f'ard him! I wish't I hadn'ta! They ain't no tellin' whut he'll do now!

**CURLY**. You f'ard him! Well then! That's all they is to it! Tomorrow, I'll get you a new h'ard hand. I'll stay on the place myself tonight, 'f you're nervous about that hound-dog. Now quit yer worryin' about it, er I'll spank ya.

> *(His manner changes. He becomes shy. He turns away, unable to meet LAUREY's eyes as he asks the question.)*

Hey, while I think of it – how – how 'bout marryin' me?

> *(LAUREY, confused, turns away, too. They are back to back.)*

**LAUREY**. Gracious, whut'd I wanta marry you fer?

**CURLY**. Well, couldn't you meybbe think of some reason why you might?

**LAUREY**. *(Crosses left.)* I cain't think of nuthin' right now, hardly.

**CURLY**. *(Following her.)* Laurey, please, ma'am – marry me. I – don't know whut I'm gonna do if you – if you don't.

**LAUREY**. *(Touched.)* Curly – why, I'll marry you – 'f you want me to...

*(They kiss.)*

**CURLY**. I'll be the happiest man alive soon as we're married. Oh, I got to learn to be a farmer, I see that! Quit a-thinkin' about throwin' a rope, and start in to git my hands blistered a new way! Oh, things is changin' right and left! Buy up mowin' machines, cut down the prairies! Shoe yer horses, drag them plows under the sod! They're gonna make a state outa this territory, they gonna put it in the Union! Country's a-changin', got to change with it! Bring up a pair of boys, new stock, to keep up 'th the way way things is goin' in this here crazy country! Now I got you to he'p me – I'll 'mount to sumpin yit! Oh, I 'member the first time I ever seen you. It was at the fair. You was a-ridin' that gray filly of Blue Starr's, and I says to someone – "Who's that skinny little thing with a bang hanging down on her forehead?"

**LAUREY**. Yeow, I 'member. You was riding broncs that day.

**CURLY**. That's right.

**LAUREY**. And one of 'em th'owed you.

**CURLY**. That's – did not th'ow me!

**LAUREY**. Guess you jumped off, then.

**CURLY**. Shore I jumped off.

**LAUREY**. Yeow, you shore did.

*(**CURLY** kisses her.)*

**[MUSIC NO. 24 "PEOPLE WILL SAY WE'RE IN LOVE (REPRISE)"]**

**CURLY**. *(Speaking over music.)* Hey! 'F there's anybody out around this yard 'at c'n hear my voice, I'd like fer you to know that Laurey Williams is my girl.

**LAUREY.** Curly!

**CURLY.** And she's went and got me to ast her to marry me!

**LAUREY.** They'll hear you all the way to Catoosie!

**CURLY.** Let 'em!

LET PEOPLE SAY WE'RE IN LOVE!
WHO KEERS WHUT HAPPENS NOW!

**LAUREY.**

JIST KEEP YOUR HAND IN MINE.
YOUR HAND FEELS SO GRAND IN MINE –

**CURLY & LAUREY.**

LET PEOPLE SAY WE'RE IN LOVE!
STARLIGHT LOOKS WELL ON US,
LET THE STARS BEAM FROM ABOVE,
WHO CARES IF THEY TELL ON US?
LET PEOPLE SAY WE'RE IN LOVE!

*(Lights fade to black.)*

## [MUSIC NO. 25 "CHANGE OF SCENE (OPTIONAL)"]

*(ALI HAKIM enters with ADO ANNIE.)*

**ALI HAKIM.** I'll say good-bye here, baby.

**ADO ANNIE.** Cain't y'even stay to drink to Curly and Laurey?

**ALI HAKIM.** *(Shaking his head.)* Time for the lonely gypsy to go back to the open road.

**ADO ANNIE.** Wisht I was goin' – nen you wouldn't be so lonely.

**ALI HAKIM.** Look, Ado Annie, there is a man I know who loves you like nothing ever loved nobody.

**ADO ANNIE.** *Ali!*

**ALI HAKIM.** A man who will stick to you all your life. And that's the man for you – Will Parker.

**ADO ANNIE.** *(Recovering from surprise.)* Oh....yeah...well, I like Will a lot.

**ALI HAKIM.** He is a fine fellow. Strong like an ox. Young and handsome.

**ADO ANNIE.** I love him, all right, I guess.

**ALI HAKIM.** Of course you do! And you love those clear blue eyes of his, and the way his mouth wrinkles up when he smiles –

**ADO ANNIE.** Do you love him too?

**ALI HAKIM.** I love him because he will make my Ado Annie happy.

> *(He kisses **ADO ANNIE**'s hand.)*

Good-bye, my baby.

> *(He starts to leave toward stage left, then turns.)*

I will show you how we say good-bye in Persia.

> *(He takes her hand, extending her arm palm up, pushes back her sleeve, and kisses her upturned wrist. He progresses up her arm, accelerating his kisses. He continues kissing her neck as he crosses behind her. He then twirls her around into a low embrace with her head stage left and plants a kiss on her lips. He then sets her on her feet in her original position.)*

**ADO ANNIE.** *(Wistfully as he releases her.)* That was good-bye?

**ALI HAKIM.** We have an old song in Persia. It says
"ONE GOODBYE...
...is never enough."

> *(He twirls her and gives her a long kiss. **WILL** enters from left and stands still and stunned. He slowly awakes to action and starts moving toward them, but then **ALI** starts to talk and **WILL** stops again, surprised even more by what he hears than by what he saw.)*

I am glad you will marry such a wonderful man as this Will Parker. You deserve a fine man and you got one.

> *(**WILL** is about to grab **ALI** by the scruff of the neck.)*

**ADO ANNIE.** *(Still in* **ALI***'s embrace, she looks up and sees* **WILL** *above her.)* Hello, Will. Ali is sayin' good-bye.

**ALI HAKIM.** *(Immediately setting* **ADO ANNIE** *back on her feet.)* Ah, Will! I want to say good-bye to you, too.

*(Starting to embrace him.)*

**WILL.** No, you don't. I just saw the last one.

**ALI HAKIM.** *(Patting* **WILL** *on the cheek.)* Ah, you were made for each other!

*(He pulls* **ADO ANNIE** *close to him with one arm and puts the other hand affectionately on* **WILL***'s shoulder.)*

Be good to her, Will.

*(Giving* **ADO ANNIE** *a squeeze.)*

And you be good to him!

*(Smiling disarmingly at* **WILL***.)*

You don't mind? I am a friend of the family now?

*(He gives* **ADO ANNIE** *a little kiss on the cheek.)*

**WILL.** Did you say you was goin'?

**ALI HAKIM.** Yes. I must. Back to the open road. A poor gypsy. Good-bye, my baby –

*(Smiling back at* **WILL** *before he kisses* **ADO ANNIE,** *pointing to himself.)*

Friend of the family.

*(Pushing* **WILL** *aside.)*

I'll show you how we say good-bye in my country.

*(***ADO ANNIE** *prepares for another Persian good-bye.* **ALI** *moves toward her, but* **WILL** *grabs him by the back of his collar.* **ALI** *smiles ingratiatingly.)*

Persian good-bye.

*(***WILL** *tosses* **ALI** *stage left, away from* **ANNIE***.)*

Lucky fellow! I wish it was me she was marrying instead of you.

**WILL.** It don't seem to make an awful lot of difference.

**ALI.** Well, back on the open road, the lonely gypsy.

> *(He sings a snatch of the Persian song as he exits, improvising on the words, "Oh, the open road!" As he disappears,* **ADO ANNIE** *runs after him, waving good-bye.)*

**WILL.** You ain't goin' to think of that ole peddler anymore, air you?

**ADO ANNIE.** Course not. Never think of no one less'n he's with me.

**WILL.** Then I'm never goin' to leave yer side.

**ADO ANNIE.** Even if you don't, even if you never go away on a trip er nuthin', cain't you – onct in a while – give me one of them Persian good-byes?

**WILL.** Persian good-bye? Why that ain't nuthin' like a Oklahoma hello!

> *(He places her hands so that she is holding on to his neck, grabs her by the waist, and slides her legs between his, giving her a long kiss. After the kiss, she looks up at him, supreme contentment in her voice.)*

**ADO ANNIE.** Hello, Will!

> *(Blackout.)*

**[MUSIC NO. 26 "CHANGE OF SCENE"]**

## Scene Three
## The Back of Laurey's Farmhouse

*(The back of Laurey's farmhouse. Shouts, cheers, and laughter are heard behind the curtain, continuing as it rises. At Rise:* **CARNES** *and* **IKE** *walking down center from up right.* **CARNES** *carries a lantern.)*

**IKE.** Well, Andrew, why ain't you back of the barn gettin' drunk with us? Never see you stay so sober at a weddin' party.

**CARNES.** Been skeered all night. Skeered 'at Jud Fry ud come up and start for Curly.

**IKE.** Why, Jud Fry's been out of the territory for three weeks.

**CARNES.** He's back. See him at Claremore last night, drunk as a lord!

*(Immediately a loud whoop is heard, and the crowd starts to pour in.* **IKE** *and* **CARNES** *move down left continuing their conversation but are drowned out by the shouts and laughter of the* **CROWD** *as they fill the stage.* **LAUREY**, *wearing her mother's wedding dress, enters from the house along with* **CURLY** *and* **AUNT ELLER**.*)*

**SLIM.** Let's have three cheers for the happy couple. Hip-hip –

**CROWD.** Hooray!

**SLIM.** Hip-hip –

**CROWD.** Hooray!

**SLIM.** Hip-hip –

**CROWD.** Hooray!

*(As* **LAUREY** *prepares to throw her bouquet, the* **GIRLS** *leave their respective beaus and rush toward the porch to catch it.* **LAUREY** *throws*

*the bouquet, and one of the* **GIRLS** *catches it,*
*after which they return to their beaus.)*

**IKE.** Say Curly, wuz you skeered when the preacher said that about do you take this 'ere womern?

**CURLY.** I wuz skeered he wouldn't say it.

## [MUSIC NO. 27 "OKLAHOMA"]

**LAUREY.** I wuz afraid Curly'd back out on me.

**AUNT ELLER.**

    THEY COULDN'T PICK A BETTER TIME TO START IN LIFE!

**IKE.**

    IT AIN'T TOO EARLY AND IT AIN'T TOO LATE.

**LAUREY.**

    STARTIN' AS A FARMER WITH A BRAND NEW WIFE –

**CURLY.**

    SOON BE LIVIN' IN A BRAND NEW STATE!

**ALL.**

    BRAND NEW STATE
    GONNA TREAT YOU GREAT!

**FRED.**

    GONNA GIVE YOU BARLEY, CARROTS AND PERTATERS –

**CORD ELAM.** *(Parlando.)*

    PASTURE FOR THE CATTLE –

**CARNES.** *(Parlando.)*

    SPINACH AND TERMAYTERS!

**AUNT ELLER.**

    FLOWERS ON THE PRAIRIE WHERE THE JUNE BUGS ZOOM –

**IKE.**

    PLEN'Y OF AIR AND PLEN'Y OF ROOM –

**FRED.**

    PLEN'Y OF ROOM TO SWING A ROPE!

**AUNT ELLER.**

    PLEN'Y OF HEART AND PLEN'Y OF HOPE...

**CURLY.**

    OKLAHOMA,

WHERE THE WIND COMES SWEEPIN' DOWN THE PLAIN,
AND THE WAVIN' WHEAT
CAN SURE SMELL SWEET
WHEN THE WIND COMES RIGHT BEHIND THE RAIN.

OKLAHOMA,
EV'RY NIGHT MY HONEY LAMB AND I
SIT ALONE AND TALK
AND WATCH A HAWK
MAKIN' LAZY CIRCLES IN THE SKY.

WE KNOW WE BELONG TO THE LAND,
AND THE LAND WE BELONG TO IS GRAND!
AND WHEN WE SAY:

**ALL.**

YEOW! A-YIP-I-O-EE-AY!

**CURLY.**

WE'RE ONLY SAYIN',
"YOU'RE DOIN' FINE, OKLAHOMA!
OKLAHOMA, O.K.!"

> (*The* **FULL COMPANY** *now joins in a refrain immediately following this one, singing with infectious enthusiasm. A special and stirring vocal arrangement.*)

**ALL.**

OKLAHOMA,
WHERE THE WIND COMES SWEEPIN' DOWN THE PLAIN,
(OKLAHOMA!)

AND THE WAVIN' WHEAT
CAN SURE SMELL SWEET
WHEN THE WIND COMES RIGHT BEHIND THE RAIN.

OKLAHOMA,
EV'RY NIGHT MY HONEY LAMB AND I
(EV'RY NIGHT WE)
SIT ALONE AND TALK
AND WATCH A HAWK
MAKIN' LAZY CIRCLES IN THE SKY.

WE KNOW WE BELONG TO THE LAND,

(YOHO!)
AND THE LAND WE BELONG TO IS GRAND!
YIPPY YI!
YIPPY YI!
YIPPY YI!
YIPPY YI!
YIPPY YI!
YIPPY YI!

AND WHEN WE SAY:
YEOW! A-YIP-I-O-EE-AY!
WE'RE ONLY SAYIN',
"YOU'RE DOIN' FINE, OKLAHOMA!
OKLAHOMA,
(YOU'RE)
O.K.!"

OKLA-
HOMA!
OKLA-
HOMA!
OKLA-
HOMA!
OKLA-
HOMA!
OKLA-
HOMA!
OKLA-

*(The "Oklahomas" continue as the rest sing.)*

WE KNOW WE BELONG TO THE LAND,
AND THE LAND WE BELONG TO IS GRAND!
AND WHEN WE SAY:
YEOW! A-YIP-I-O-EE-AY!
WE'RE ONLY SAYIN',
"YOU'RE DOIN' FINE, OKLAHOMA!
OKLAHOMA, O. K. L. A. H. O. M. A!"
OKLAHOMA!

*(Shouted.)*

YEOW!

## [MUSIC NO. 28 "OKLAHOMA (ENCORE)"]

OKLAHOMA,
WHERE THE WIND COMES SWEEPIN' DOWN THE PLAIN,
(OKLAHOMA!)

WHERE THE WAVIN' WHEAT
CAN SURE SMELL SWEET
WHEN THE WIND COMES RIGHT BEHIND THE RAIN.

OKLAHOMA,
EV'RY NIGHT MY HONEY LAMB AND I
(EV'RY NIGHT WE)
SIT ALONE AND TALK
AND WATCH A HAWK
MAKIN' LAZY CIRCLES IN THE SKY.

OKLA-
HOMA!
OKLA-
HOMA!
OKLA-
HOMA!
OKLA-
HOMA!
OKLA-
HOMA!
OKLA-

*(The "Oklahomas" continue as the rest sing.)*

WE KNOW WE BELONG TO THE LAND,
AND THE LAND WE BELONG TO IS GRAND!
AND WHEN WE SAY:
YEOW! A-YIP-I-O-EE-AY!
WE'RE ONLY SAYIN',
"YOU'RE DOIN' FINE, OKLAHOMA!
OKLAHOMA, O. K. L. A. H. O. M. A!"
OKLAHOMA!

*(Shouted.)*

YEOW!

*(After number.)*

**CURLY.** Hey! Y'better hurry into that other dress! Gotta git goin' in a minnit!

(**LAUREY** *exits into the house.*)

**AUNT ELLER.** You hurry and pack yer own duds! They're layin' all over my room.

(*She follows* **LAUREY** *into the house.*)

**CURLY.** Hey, Will! Would you hitch the team to the surrey fer me?

**WILL.** Shore will! Have it up in a jiffy!

(*He runs off.* **CURLY** *exits into the house.* **CORD ELAM** *runs over to the door. The manner of the group of* **MEN** *that surrounds the door becomes mysterious. Their voices are low and their talk is punctuated with winks and nudges.*)

**IKE.** (*To* **CORD.**) He's gone upstairs.

**CORD ELAM.** Yeah.

(**CORD ELAM** *and the* **MEN** *join* **IKE** *by the door, and then all get into a huddle. The* **GIRLS** *cross to the* **MEN** *but are shooed away. The* **MEN** *whisper and slip quietly off, except for* **CARNES.** *The* **GIRLS** *break toward* **CARNES** *as* **ADO ANNIE** *crosses to him.*)

**ADO ANNIE.** Whut you goin' to do, Paw? Give Laurey and Curly a shivoree? I wisht you wouldn't.

**CARNES.** Aw, it's a good old-fashioned custom. Never hurt anybody. You women jist keep outa the way. Vamoose!

(*The* **GIRLS** *all talk at once.*)

Stop gabbin' about it!

(*He exits up right, leaving only* **WOMEN** *on the stage.*)

**ADO ANNIE.** Seems like they's times when men ain't got no need for womern.

**SECOND GIRL.** Well, they's times when womern ain't got no need for men.

**ADO ANNIE.** Yeow, but who wants to be dead?

> (**GERTIE**'s *well-known laugh is heard, off right.*)

**ELLEN.** Gertie!

> (**GERTIE** *enters.*)

**ADO ANNIE.** Thought you was in Bushyhead.

**GERTIE.** (*Smugly.*) Just come from there.

**ELLEN.** Too bad you missed Laurey's wedding.

**GERTIE.** Been havin' one of my own.

**ELLEN.** Lands! Who'd you marry? Where is he?

**ADO ANNIE.** (*Looking off.*) Is that him?

**GERTIE.** (*Triumphantly.*) That's him!

> (*All look off right.* **ALI HAKIM** *enters, dejected, sheepish, dispirited, a ghost of the man he was.*)

**ADO ANNIE.** Ali Hakim!

**GERTIE.** Did you see my ring, girls?

> (*The* **GIRLS** *surround* **GERTIE** *to admire and exclaim.* **ALI** *and* **ADO ANNIE** *are left apart from the group.*)

**ADO ANNIE.** How long you been married?

**ALI HAKIM.** Four days.

> (**GERTIE**'s *laugh is heard from the group.* **ALI** *winces.*)

Four days with that laugh should count like a golden wedding.

**ADO ANNIE.** But if you married her, you musta wanted to.

**ALI HAKIM.** Sure I wanted to. I wanted to marry her when I saw the moonlight shining on the barrel of her father's shotgun! I thought it would be better to be alive.

> (*A short laugh from* **GERTIE**.)

**ALI HAKIM.** Now, I ain't so sure.

**GERTIE.** *(Coming out of group.)* Ali ain't goin' to travel around the country no more. I decided he orta settle down in Bushyhead and run Papa's store.

*(***WILL*** enters from left.)*

**ADO ANNIE.** Hey! Will! D'you hear the news? Gertie married the peddler.

**WILL.** *(To* **ALI.***)* Mightly glad to hear that, peddler-man.

*(Turning to* **GERTIE** *and getting an idea.)*

I think I orta kiss the bride.

*(He goes toward* **GERTIE,** *then looks back at* **ALI.***)*

Friend of the fambly...remember? Hey, Gertie, have you ever had an Oklahoma hello?

*(He starts to give her an "Oklahoma hello."* **ADO ANNIE** *rushes in and pushes* **WILL** *across to the side. She then turns back and takes a swing at* **GERTIE,** *who ducks under her arm.* **GERTIE** *grabs her around the waist, but* **ADO ANNIE** *gets hold of* **GERTIE***'s hair and swings her round.* **GERTIE** *pulls* **ADO ANNIE***'s skirt up over her head and begins to flee off left with the other* **GIRLS** *screaming.* **ADO ANNIE** *scrambles to right herself, then chases after* **GERTIE.** **WILL** *is about to follow when he is called back by* **ALI.***)*

**ALI HAKIM.** Hey! Where you goin'?

**WILL.** I'm goin' to stop Ado Annie from killin' yer wife.

**ALI HAKIM.** *(Grabbing* **WILL***'s arm.)* Mind yer own business!

*(He leads* **WILL** *off. The stage is empty and quiet. A* **MAN** *sneaks on, then another, then more. Cautiously, a few advance on the house while others spread across the stage, huddling in groups. One of the more agile climbs up a trellis and looks in the window of the second*

*floor. He suppresses a laugh, leans down, and reports to the others. There are suppressed giggles and snorts. He takes another peek, then comes down and whispers to them. The joke is passed from one group to the other; they are doubled up with laughter. Then, at a signal from one, they all start to pound on tin pans with spoons and set up a terrific din.)*

**AUNT ELLER.** *(Coming to the window with a lamp in her hand.)* Whut you doin' down there, makin' all thet racket, you bunch o' pig-stealers?

**FRED.** *(Shouting up.)* Come on down peaceable, Laurey, sugar!

**IKE.** And you too, you curly-headed cowboy.

**CORD ELAM.** With the dimple on yer chin!

**IKE.** Come on, fellers, let's git 'em down!

*(Three of the MEN run into the house. Those outside toss up straw dolls.)*

**MEN.** Hey, Laurey! Here's a girl baby fer you! And here's a baby boy! Here's twins!

*(CURLY is pulled from the house and hoisted on the shoulders of his friends. LAUREY and AUNT ELLER come out of the house. All are in high spirits. It is a good-natured hazing. Now JUD enters up left. Everyone becomes quiet and still, sensing trouble.)*

**JUD.** Weddin' party still goin' on? Glad I ain't too late. Got a present fer the groom. But first I want to kiss the bride.

*(He starts for LAUREY. CURLY pulls him back.)*

An' here's my present fer you!

*(He socks CURLY. The fight starts, with the CROWD moving around the two men. The fight continues to its climax, at which point JUD pulls a knife and goes for CURLY. CURLY grabs his arm and succeeds in throwing him.*

JUD *falls on his knife, groans, and lies still. The* **CROWD** *surges toward his motionless body.)*

**CURLY.** Look – look at him! Fell on his own knife!

*(He backs away, shaken, limp. Some of the* **MEN** *bend over the prostrate form.)*

**SLIM.** Roll him over somebody.

**MEN.** *(Through* **SLIM**'*s next line they overlap the following ad-libs.)* Don't tetch him.

What's the matter?

Don't you tetch it!

Turn him over – he's breathin', ain't he?

Feel his heart.

How'd it happen?

**FRED.** Whut'll we do? Ain't he all right?

**SLIM.** 'S he just stunned?

**CORD ELAM.** Git away, some of you. Let me look at him.

*(He bends down, the* **MEN** *crowding around. The* **WOMEN**, *huddled together, look on, struck with horror.* **CURLY** *has slumped back away from the crowd like a sick man.* **LAUREY** *looks at* **CURLY**, *dazed, a question in her eyes.)*

**LAUREY.** Curly – is he – ?

**CURLY.** Don't say anythin'.

**LAUREY.** It cain't be that-a-way.

**CURLY.** I didn't go to.

**LAUREY.** *Cain't be!* Like that – to happen to us.

**CORD ELAM.** *(Getting up.)* Cain't do a thing now. Try to get him to a doctor, but I don't know –

**SLIM.** Here, some of you, carry him over to my rig. I'll drive him over to Doc Tyler's.

**CORD ELAM.** Quick! I'm afraid it's too late.

*(The* **MEN** *lift* **JUD** *up and carry him off toward the road.)*

**MEN.** *(Ad-libbing as* **JUD** *is carried off.)* Handle him easy! Don't shake him!

Hold on to him careful there!

**CURLY.** *(To* **LAUREY** *and* **AUNT ELLER.)** I got to go see if there's anythin' c'n be done fer him.

> *(He kisses* **LAUREY.***)*

Take keer of her, Aunt Eller.

> *(He exits.)*

**AUNT ELLER.** Mebber it's better fer you and Curly not t'go 'way tonight.

> *(She breaks off, realizing how feeble this must sound.)*

**LAUREY.** *(As if she hadn't heard* **AUNT ELLER.***)* I don't see why this had to happen, when everythin' was so fine.

**AUNT ELLER.** Don't let yer mind run on it.

**LAUREY.** Cain't fergit, I tell you. Never will!

**AUNT ELLER.** 'At's all right, Laurey baby. If you cain't fergit, jist don't try to, honey. Oh, lots of things happen to folks. Sickness, er bein' pore and hungry even – bein' old and afeared to die. That's the way it is – cradle to grave. And you can stand it. They's one way. You gotta be hearty, you got to be. You cain't deserve the sweet and tender in life less'n you're tough.

**LAUREY.** I – I wisht I was the way you are.

**AUNT ELLER.** Fiddlesticks! Scrawy and old? You couldn't h'ar me to be the way I am!

> *(***LAUREY** *laughs through her tears.)*

**LAUREY.** Oh, whut ud I do 'thout you, you're sich a crazy!

**AUNT ELLER.** *(Hugging* **LAUREY.***)* Shore's you're borned!

> *(She breaks off as* **CURLY** *enters with* **CORD ELAM, CARNES,** *and a few others. Their manner is sober. Some of the* **WOMEN** *come out of the house to hear what the men have to say.)*

**CORD ELAM.** They're takin' Jud over to Dave Tyler's till the mornin'.

**AUNT ELLER.** Is he – alive?

> (**CORD ELAM** *shakes his head to indicate "no."*)

**CURLY.** Laurey honey, Cord Elam here, he's a fed'ral marshal, y'know. And he thinks I orta give myself up – tonight, he thinks.

**LAUREY.** Tonight!

**AUNT ELLER.** Why yer train leaves Claremore in twenty minutes.

**CORD ELAM.** Best thing is fer Curly to go of his own accord and tell the judge.

**AUNT ELLER.** *(To* **CARNES.***)* Why, you're the judge, ain't you, Andrew?

**CARNES.** Yes, but –

**LAUREY.** *(Urging* **CURLY** *forward.)* Well, tell him now and git it over with.

**CORD ELAM.** 'T wouldn't be proper. You have to do it in court.

**AUNT ELLER.** Oh, fiddlesticks. Le's do it here and say we did it in court.

**CORD ELAM.** We can't do that. That's breaking the law.

**AUNT ELLER.** Well, le's not break the law. Le's just bend it a little. C'mon, Andrew, and start the trial. We ain't got but a few minnits.

**CORD ELAM.** Andrew – I got to protest.

**CARNES.** Oh, shet yer trap. We can give the boy a fair trial without lockin' him up on his weddin' night! Here's the long and short of it. First I got to ask you: Whut's your plea?

> (**CURLY** *doesn't answer.* **CARNES** *prompts him.)*

'At means why did you do it?

**CURLY.** Why'd I do it? Cuz he'd been pesterin' Laurey and I always said someday I'd –

**CARNES.** Just a minnit! Just a minnit! Don't let yer tongue wobble around in yer mouth like 'at... Listen to my question. Whut happened tonight 'at made you kill him.

**CURLY.** Why he come at me with a knife and – and –

**CARNES.** And you had to defend yerself, didn't you?

**CURLY.** Why, yes – and furthermore...

**CARNES.** Never mind the furthermores – the plea is self-defense –

(*The* **WOMEN** *start to chatter.*)

Quiet! Now is there a witness who saw this happen?

**MEN.** (*All at once.*) I seen it.

Shore did.

Self-defense all right.

Tried to stab him 'th a frog sticker.

**CORD ELAM.** (*Shaking his hand.*) I feel funny about this, Andrew. I shore feel funny.

**AUNT ELLER.** You'll feel funny when I tell yer wife you're carryin' on 'th another womern?

**CORD ELAM.** I ain't carryin' on 'th no one.

**AUNT ELLER.** Mebber not, but you'll shore feel funny when I tell yer *wife* you air.

(*Boisterous laughter.*)

**CORD ELAM.** Laugh, all you like, but as a fed'ral marshal –

**SKIDMORE.** Oh, shet up about being marshal! We ain't goin' to let ya send the boy to jail on his weddin' night. We just ain't goin' to *let* ya. So shet up!

(*This firm and conclusive statement is cheered and applauded.*)

**SLIM.** C'mon fellers! Let's pull them to their train in Curly's surrey! And we'll be the horses.

*(The* **CROWD** *begins to disperse.)*

**CARNES.** Hey, wait a minute! I ain't even told the verdick yet!

> *(Everything stops still at this unpleasant reminder.)*

**CURLY.** Well – the verdick's not guilty, ain't it?

**CARNES.** Course, but...

**LAUREY.** Well, then *say* it!

> *(***CARNES*** *starts, but the* **CROWD** *drowns him out.)*

**ALL.** Not guilty!

> *(***CURLY*** *and* **LAUREY** *run into the house. Four of the* **MEN** *run off to get the surrey.* **CARNES** *is left downstage without a "court.")*

**CARNES.** Court's adjourned!

> *(***AUNT ELLER** *laughs, crosses to bench left.* **CARNES** *joins* **AUNT ELLER***, who has sat down to rest after all this excitement.* **ADO ANNIE** *and* **WILL** *enter, holding hands soulfully.* **ADO ANNIE***'s hair is mussed, and a contented look graces her face.)*

**AUNT ELLER.** Why, Ado Annie, where on earth have you been?

**ADO ANNIE.** Will and me had a misunderstandin'. But he explained it fine.

> *(***ADO ANNIE** *and* **WILL** *go upstage, and now tell-tale wisps of straw are seen clinging to* **ADO ANNIE***'s back. Two or three* **YOUNG GIRLS** *run after them, giggling and pointing at the straw.)*

**[MUSIC NO. 29 "FINALE ULTIMO"]**

> *(Amid shouts and laughter, the surrey is pulled on. The younger* **BOYS** *and* **GIRLS**

*examine it with great delight as it is being positioned. The* **CROWD** *sings lustily as* **IKE** *speaks over them.)*

**ALL.**

I GOT A BEAUTIFUL FEELIN'
EV'RYTHIN'S GOIN' MY WAY.

**IKE.** Hey, there, bride and groom, y'ready?

**CURLY.** *(Running out of the house with* **LAUREY.***)* Here we come.

*(There is much movement as* **LAUREY** *kisses* **ADO ANNIE, IKE,** *and* **CARNES** *while* **CURLY** *shakes hands with* **CARNES, IKE,** *and* **WILL.** *Finally,* **LAUREY** *hugs* **AUNT ELLER,** *and* **CURLY** *lifts her into the surrey. Everyone else sings.)*

**ALL.**

OH, WHAT A BEAUTIFUL MORNIN',
OH, WHAT A BEAUTIFUL DAY!
I GOT A BEAUTIFUL FEELIN'

*(***LAUREY** *is helped into the surrey by* **CURLY.***)*

EV'RYTHIN'S GOIN' MY WAY...

*(***LAUREY** *and* **CURLY** *are seated in the surrey.)*

OH, WHAT A BEAUTIFUL DAY.

*(On "Oh" of the last line,* **MEN** *start to pull the surrey off. Everybody waves as they fall in place, following.* **CURLY** *and* **LAUREY** *wave through the back of the surrey as the curtain falls.)*

*(As the music of "People Will Say We're In Love" begins, the curtain rises. The* **COMPANY** *has regrouped in an old-fashioned tableau, as if they were posing for a photograph. After the first twelve bars of music, they sing. As they sing, they break the formality of the tableau.* **LAUREY** *and* **CURLY** *leave the surrey and come down center front.)*

**ALL.**

PEOPLE WILL SAY WE'RE IN LOVE.

DON'T START COLLECTING THINGS –
GIVE ME MY ROSE AND MY GLOVE.

SWEETHEART, THEY'RE SUSPECTING THINGS –
PEOPLE WILL SAY WE'RE IN LOVE!

*(Curtain.)*

# The End